T5-DHH-700

THE AWAKENING WATER

By the same author

*

THE PALE INVADERS

THE AWAKENING WATER

•

G. R. KESTEVEN

HASTINGS HOUSE, PUBLISHERS

NEW YORK

Published in the United States of America in 1979 by
Hastings House, Publishers, Inc.

Published in Great Britain by Chatto & Windus, Ltd.

Library of Congress Cataloging in Publication Data

Crosher, G. R.
The awakening water.

Summary: After the devastation of 1997, 13-year-old
Watford Nine John accidentally breaks out of the regimen
imposed by the Party and decides not to return.
[1. Science fiction] I. Title.
PZ7.C8823Aw 1979 [Fic] 78-27186
ISBN 0-8038-0471-7

Printed in the United States of America

CONTENTS

1

Meeting at a Spring

WATFORD Nine John first tasted the awakening water on an April day which began with cool, low mistiness and then, about mid-morning, cleared to allow the sun to beat down with almost summer warmth. Until that day he had lived his thirteen years aware of little but the round of working and sleeping.

With the other boys of his House, John had spent the morning earthing up the early potatoes. Hoe in hand he had plodded along his allotted rows, his eyes on the earth as he scraped it up to form the ridge covering the first darkly green shoots. He had not noticed that he was working a little less slowly than the other boys so that when Hemel Martin, the duty-man for the day, called a halt John was already well across the field. As he straightened his back, John became aware that a sycamore just beyond the fence had dropped a patch of cool-looking shade just inside the field, only a dozen or so paces away, and the sight made him conscious of the sun's warmth. But with the other boys he trudged back to where, in the middle of the field's sunlit expanse, Hemel Martin was standing, handing out the oat-cakes. Not until the duty-man said that he had forgotten the water cask and the beakers did John feel his mouth's dryness.

Duty-man Martin looked from one to another of the dozen boys, each turning towards him a round-eyed, slightly disappointed face. 'I didn't know it was going to be so hot,' he said in a flat, heavy tone. He turned to look along the field with its newly raised ridges. 'You've done well,' he added, his voice carrying no hint of appreciation.

'It's not worth sending back for the water. You'll be finished in an hour.'

Only on John's face a hint of dissatisfaction lingered. Under his bleached brows his blue eyes shadowed a little and his mouth took on a faintly discontented droop. All went on slowly chewing the oat-cakes before forcing themselves to swallow. Duty-man Martin added: 'You needn't hurry as it's turned so hot.'

John looked away from the man's almost expressionless face. Though he did not recognise it, that face was an older version of the boys', a little thinner and the skin a trace coarser but as free of the lines of age or living; and when the duty-man moved to squat between the potato-rows, he took the few paces with slow, plodding movements like those of the boys. Had John noticed, he would not have thought the similarities in any way unusual. Rarely had he seen anyone, young or old, move with alertness or look with interest; the placid, ponderous manner was as characteristic of the duty-men as of the boys. To John it appeared natural.

Only at a Celebration, at Harvest or New Year, had John seen anyone, boy or girl, duty-man or duty-woman, behave otherwise; and then, bewilderingly, all had done so. At a Celebration all the Watford Houses – except the Mothers' House – met at the Local Centre. Into the lofty building with a tower at the entrance and pointed windows in which coloured glass made pictures, the hundred or so children had been gathered. . . though, on those rare occasions, John had taken little notice of his surroundings. Like all the others, his eyes had been from the first moment on the tables with their bowls and plates of food: meats and fruit, and sweet soft foods and sweet crisp foods such as he had tasted only at Celebrations and for which he knew no name, and a white drink which the duty-women called 'milk'.

After everyone had eaten came the strangest part of the Celebration. All the boys and girls were encouraged to get up from the benches to form circles, hands held, and to go lumbering round while from within the recesses of the building came a strange, rhythmical noise. Sometimes, above the sounds of shuffling feet and the noise, a boy would shout out suddenly or a girl's shriller voice would utter a laugh. Then others would take up the unaccustomed sounds, and their faces would twist into grins, and the ponderous dance would quicken until they began to feel unnaturally easier, lighter, as if they could speed over the stone floor of the Local Centre.

By then the climax of the Celebration was nearing. Soon the rhythmical sounds would stop abruptly, and the duty-men and duty-women would be telling the boys and girls to 'settle down'. Then the District Party Leader would come in, and the young faces, their eyes again round, their mouths slightly drooping, would turn to the tall, thin figure with a mass of white hair and a face so lined and so sharpened by quick eyes that it was unlike the adult faces they knew.

With the others John had gazed on that disturbing, alert face while the District Leader told the duty-men and women and 'all you boys and girls, too' how delighted he was that the Harvest had been so good or that he hoped the New Year would 'bring better times for all of us'. Then, his bright eyes turning from the many vaguely uneasy faces, the District Leader would add a sentence or two to the duty-men and women about the Celebration being 'almost like before nineteen ninety-seven'. Always, it seemed to John, the man had used those numbers, though their significance was beyond John's guessing. John knew only that the Celebration, the brief hours away from the House and the work, was ending. Soon the girls would be ushered by the duty-women away to their Houses, soon the boys, under their duty-men's eyes, would be filing back... though a few of the newer duty-men and women would stay behind at the Local Centre, the men unusually grinning as they watched the boys and girls go, the women's eyes shining.

Such breaks in the steady passing of work-days came only rarely, and the feeling of excitement, the awareness of being able to move quickly, to run, to shout, soon dispersed. To John the next Celebration always seemed so far ahead that he could not look forward to it. Instead, with the other boys, he plodded through what seemed an endless succession of days varied only by the tasks imposed by the seasons and the duty-men or, as today, disturbed by an unexpected change in the weather. Today, as on any day but the two or three leading to Harvest or New Year, his awareness reached no more than an hour or two ahead.

Now, as he stood munching his oat-cake and feeling the dryness of it in his throat, John knew only that he was thirsty and that the sun was hot. He stared back along the potato-row and so, after a few seconds, noticed again the patch of cool shade under the sycamore leaning over the fence. Without thought he began towards it. . . while, though it had not occurred to him to look, Duty-man Martin's head drooped as he squatted between the potato-rows.

Plodding along towards the beckoning shade, John knew that only twenty or so paces to his left the river flowed unhurriedly behind a screen of willows; but not for a moment did he think of the river-water easing his thirst. He knew how dangerous was the river. Week after week he had read about it during the two-hour-long Lesson Times with which each day ended. Sitting at the tables after the Meal had been cleared, all the boys chanted the day's story; and as the stained and thumbed books contained only a few stories, they had long become familiar to John. Each story told of some happening – 'Adventures' the book called them though the word had no meaning for John – in which a boy had earned a District Party Leader's approval by some worthy act or had suffered serious mishap from his disobedience to a duty-man's orders. One story, the only one which still stirred a trace of interest in

John's mind, told of a District Leader's van breaking down and how a boy, seeing him stranded, had run for miles to get help and so had prevented an unspecified disaster. Another story, the one which came to John as he trudged along the potato-field, told of a boy who had drunk river-water and had become infected with a sickness which made him so disobedient that he would do nothing he was told until Matron had to take him away for treatment. So embedded in John's mind had that story become that he felt nothing of the nearby river's cool temptation as he plodded towards the shade cast by the sycamore.

Reaching it, John saw that brambles spreading through the fence denied him the half-formed notion of resting in the shade. He stood a while looking at the bramble cluster, annoyance bringing only a slight contraction of his brows . . . until he noticed that, a few paces away, a tree which had once supported the fence had been blown down and so had left a gap. That sight did not at once tell him that he could push through the fence; it had never occurred to him to go beyond the confines of the familiar fields about the House. But as he stood staring vaguely down the short slope, he became aware of the shimmer of water among the rushes and tufted grass at the bottom. The sight made him lick his lips and edge towards the gap in the fence. . . and so he saw through the growth that clung to the slope, two girls crouched over the water.

John stood, staring. He assumed that they must have come from the nearby Girls' House, but the hidden hollow was not a place he would have expected to see them. And their quick movements brought a rare feeling of puzzlement and for once John's round eyes narrowed. Then he saw one of them, the smaller, dark-haired girl, scoop up water in her hands and drink.

The sight, so unexpected, made John stiffen. He realised that the girls must be – could only be – two of those strange people who lived in the woods, the Lost Ones which another story told about. That story had always baffled John for it gave no reason why there should be such people as Lost Ones. It told only that they had run away from the safety of their House, defying the duty-men's attempts to catch them and even their District Leader's orders to return. Such disobedient people, the story ended, had to live on what leaves and berries they could find until, in the depths of winter, they were forced to creep back to their House and face the Party's punishment or, sickened by cold, they perished in some lonely hiding-place.

Yet, as he stared, John became aware that the girls did not fit the story's impression of Lost Ones. As the taller, fair girl moved from behind a bush he saw no hint of a dejected, half-starved appearance; he saw, too, that though she was dressed in the usual tunic and trews, patches on them suggested that she had not come from a Girls' House. And her quick movements reminded him not of any girl he had seen at a Celebration but of the District Leader himself! For the first time in his life John felt alarmed, and had to turn away from such a disturbing sight. But he moved so clumsily that a bramble snared his foot and he tripped. With a grunted cry he fell through the gap in the fence, through a tangle of snatching twigs, down the short slope towards where the girls had been crouching over the shimmering water.

Never before had anything so sudden happened to him. For several moments John lay on his back, staring up at the sky between the branches of the trees clinging to the slope, unable to understand. At last, realising what had occurred, he squirmed round to look for the two girls. They had vanished.

John stared into the growth rising up the far slope. Nothing on it moved. For a while he lay trying to understand. Nowhere in the story about the Lost Ones had there been any suggestion that they could so speedily and so inexplicably disappear. John began to wonder if he had truly seen them. . .

The water was trickling out from the darkness under a tangle of brambles. Returning awareness of it made John lick his dry lips. He had never before seen water seeping out from under the earth; for him the sight did not link with the fearsome river – rather, it suggested some new kind of water. And, he recalled, one of the girls had drunk from its tempting clearness. He could see the pebbles over which it ran; the stream had not the greyish look of the water the duty-men provided at every meal-time.

The stream was not an arm's length from where he lay. Cautiously he reached out a hand to it, impelled by his thirst and yet unable to still an awareness that the water was strange and therefore suspect. As his fingers found the sudden coolness, a voice came to him from only a few paces across the stream: 'Go on, have a drink. It's all right!'

John snatched his hand back from the water and stared towards the sound; but only the branches and the tangle of growth met his gaze until the girl's voice came again: 'It's all right, Helen. It's only a boy dropped in for a drink!'

The joke did not penetrate John's comprehension, but the easy lightness of the voice caught at him. He glimpsed a face, small and framed with near-black hair, watching him from the darkness of a holly-bush. He caught, too, her smile; it was far more relaxed than the smiles on the girls' faces as they danced at a Celebration.

She moved almost casually out from the cover of the holly-bush, and John saw that the other girl, the fair-haired, plumper one, had been standing a pace or two behind her. The second girl's eyes were also bright with a smile as, still lying beside the stream, John stared up at them.

'What's up?' asked the smaller, dark-haired one. 'Why don't you drink it if you're thirsty? It's not doped.'

The fair girl flashed a glance at her. 'Careful, Janet,' she warned. 'There's a duty-man in the field.'

That seemed to add to the brightness in the dark-haired girl's eyes. 'What about it? He'd be much too slow!'

Their easy, quick voices were to John more puzzling

than reassuring. Never had he heard anyone talk so light-heartedly; he could not recall, in the story about Lost Ones, any hint that they spoke so. His vague imaginings had assumed such people to be always dejected and afraid. Uneasy, he looked away from the two girls, and saw again the sparkling water.

'Go on, have a drink!' urged the dark-haired one. 'We'll tell you if the duty-man's coming!'

John's thirst had returned more strongly. He looked from the water to the girl. 'Is it all right?' he ventured, and in his own ears his dull, heavy tone contrasted with the girls' easy voices.

'Of course it is!' said the dark-haired girl. 'A spring's always all right.'

Again John reached out to the water. He scooped up some in the palm of his hand, and raised it to his lips. The first, tentative sip startled him with its coldness.

'Go on! What are you scared of?'

The water had a slightly earthy taste, unlike the faint sickliness of the water he had always known. It seemed at once to penetrate the dryness in his mouth. He risked another handful, and then another. The water's refreshing coolness impelled him to squirm forward so that he could reach his mouth into the stream, could gulp up the water.

At last he raised his head, wiping the drips from his nose with the back of his hand. He heard the dark-haired girl's light laugh.

'Doesn't that make you feel better?' she asked. 'It's not that doped stuff the duty-men give you, is it?'

John stared up at them, not understanding. 'Doped stuff?' he repeated.

'Of course you don't know,' replied the girl. 'That powder that the duty-men put in the water: that's a kind of dope to keep you quiet.'

'To keep me quiet?' John asked, uncomprehending.

'Yes! Otherwise you might start thinking and trying to get back to – to things as they were before nineteen ninety-seven. That's why the Party-Leaders do it.'

John's mind had to clutch at phrases from the words she spoke so quickly. 'Nineteen ninety-seven?' he asked, aware that he had heard the numbers before.

The dark eyes showed a trace of irritation at his repeating what she said. 'You are slow! Don't you know –?'

The fair-haired girl interrupted: 'Don't be unkind, Janet. Don't forget you were like him only a few months ago. We all were once.'

'I wasn't! I couldn't have been so –'

'You were,' the fair girl insisted.

For a moment the dark one looked uneasy. Then, her voice less quick, she asked John: 'What's your name?'

'Watford Nine John.'

'Watford?' She gave a glance towards the potato-field. 'Is Watford over there?'

Again John did not understand. The word 'Watford' was part of his name, part of the names of all the boys in his House, and of the girls in their Houses, too. But this girl was speaking as if it meant more, as if it was the Houses themselves.

'What's it like?' she went on. 'Are there many old buildings left? Are there any fruit-trees among them, or any wild chickens or – or anything like that?'

'Fruit?' John asked, baffled. There were, he knew, rows of apple-trees and bushes of currants and gooseberries in the orchard behind the House. Later on he and the other boys would gather the fruit into baskets before loading them on the van which took them to the Local Centre.

'You must know what fruit are!' exclaimed the dark girl, and again John caught the annoyance in her voice. 'Are there any fruit-trees – about the old buildings, I mean. The people used to grow them sometimes near their homes and there are still some left. . .'

The other girl said gently: 'He doesn't understand.'

John tried to think what the dark-haired girl could mean. She spoke of buildings being Watford. He could recall having seen, as they walked to a Celebration, fragments of walls on either side of the roadway. So broken were those that he remembered, and so shrouded in trees and bushes and nettle-thickets, that it had never occurred to him that people might once have lived in them.

The fair-haired girl was looking across the stream to the break in the fence. 'They're getting back to work,' she said with a glance at John.

He stared at her, not realising that from her higher viewpoint she could see into the potato-field. The girl went on: 'You'd better be getting back or the duty-men will come looking for you.'

John started at that, got up and began to scramble up the slope down which he had fallen. He heard the dark-haired girl's laugh.

'Sh, Janet!' warned the fair one. 'They'll hear you!'

'He looks so funny, so clumsy! And why hurry?'

Clutching a low branch to hold himself on the slope, John looked back at them. From the darkness under the holly-tree, the dark-haired girl's voice reached him. 'What are you afraid of? What does it matter if the duty-man sees you? You can say you've been behind a tree or – or something!'

'Behind a tree?' John repeated, and again his voice sounded heavy in his own ears.

'Yes, been to the loo, sort of!' Then with another light laugh, she seemed to dissolve into the growth on the far slope. John stared after her for several moments, unable to understand how she – and the other girl, too – could so vanish.

It was not until he had struggled up to the gap in the fence that John understood what the girl had meant. Her cunning amazed him; he would never, he knew, have thought of such an excuse for leaving the field.

The other boys were already bending over their hoeing. For a moment after he had taken up his hoe, John stood blinking at them; it was as if for the first time he saw the emptiness on all their faces, and the slow, laboured movements that were common to all the boys. It was the impression of a moment before, seeing Duty-man Martin begin towards him, John bent to the work.

The duty-man lumbered up to him. 'Are you all right?' he asked, and John noticed the slow, dull voice.

John nodded; and then, remembering: 'I just went behind a tree.'

The man appeared not to understand, nor to catch the faint glint of cunning that had come into John's eyes. 'Are you sure you're all right?' he asked. 'Perhaps it's the sun. It's so hot, suddenly.'

John felt again the sun's warmth, and he remembered how Watford James who always worked next to him, had one day last Harvest-gathering become so faint that he had had to be carried back to the House. The duty-men had spoken of sending for Matron; but James had recovered in time.

John did not feel faint. 'I'm all right,' he said again. He felt, strangely, more awake than usual as if somehow he had caught a little, just a little, of the girls' quickness. Surely such a feeling could not have been brought by the sun's warmth?

2

The Strange Sickness

FOR the first time in his thirteen years, John did not fall asleep within moments of lying on his bunk. Even after the Dormitory light had been turned out, he lay awake. The meeting with the two girls, the strange alertness of them, seemed to be still stirring in his mind and had not, as so often happened with memories, become speedily so blurred as to lose reality. He could still remember the dark-haired one's bright eyes, could hear her rushing talk and the fair girl's gentler voice. . . though their words were no longer clear.

As he lay with his eyes closed from habit, John's hearing caught the sounds of the other boys in the room. He could not recall having ever before noticed the different sounds of breathing. Now he could distinguish the whispered breaths of James in the bunk below from Jonah's soft grunts from the next bunk, and a faint hissing from Jasper. He tried listening to the boys whose bunks jutted out from the opposite wall. Being a year older than himself, their names began with I. With a feeling of surprise John realised he could tell the difference between Isaac's deep breathing and Ivor's slow murmurs. Without risking raising his head, John reached his hearing to the fifteen-year-olds beyond them, and felt sure he could distinguish Harry's faint wheeze from Howard's steady breaths.

The unusualness both of being awake at such a time and of using his hearing in such a novel way seemed to hold off sleep. Or could it be partly the effect of the strange water he had drunk at the stream? Curiously, he could still recall its refreshing coolness; and, since then, John had drunk nothing. He had not thought to avoid the beaker that was, as always, set at his place at the meal-table; it was just that he had not felt thirsty and when James, sitting as usual beside him, had asked if he did not want the water, John had said 'no', and James had gulped it down. Not until now did he realise that he had never before done such a thing and, almost as surprising, the duty-man had apparently not noticed.

Now, nearly three hours later and after slow-passing Lesson Time – and tonight's story had been the too-familiar one about the boy rescuing a duty-man trapped in a burning building and being recommended to become a duty-man himself when he was old enough – John began to feel thirsty again. He would, he assumed, have to wait until morning. . . or would he? The Meal's vegetable stew had left a saltiness in his mouth; surely if he told the duty-man he could not sleep he would be given a drink.

John raised his head and looked around the room. None of the shapes, wrapped in steady sleep, stirred, though the wheezing from the bunk nearest the door changed tone a little. Peering through the darkness, John identified the sleeper as Harry who had the bunk where Eric used to sleep.

At that recollection, John felt a trace of puzzlement. As far as he could remember, he had not thought of Eric for months or years, not since the evening when, as the boys filed into the Dormitory, the duty-men had realised that Eric was missing. There had followed an evening of unusual activity about the House; and then through two or three days there had been comings and goings, Matron appearing twice to urge her bulk about the place and, on the second evening, the District Party Leader arriving. John could dimly recall the boys of Eric's year waiting outside the duty-men's room, and hearing that the Leader was inside. He could recall more clearly the Leader's eyes as he had walked about the House, making sharp suggestions to the duty-men trying to keep pace with him.

And at some time during those confusing days strange duty-men had been seen about the fields around the House, appearing to be searching.

And then, abruptly, Eric's disappearance seemed to have been forgotten. The even pattern of work was resumed, and John overheard one duty-man saying to another that, anyway, Eric would have been leaving the House soon. . .

Beyond that John's memory did not go. Until now, it was as if a mistiness had wrapped about the incident, blotting it out of his mind. Never once since then could he recall having thought of Eric and now he could not remember what the boy had looked like. It was almost as if Eric had never been there, had never slept in the bunk now used by Harry.

Recollection of Eric seemed to increase John's sleeplessness; and that, in turn, sharpened his thirst. He risked sitting up. Again no one stirred. He edged himself over the side of the bunk and dropped to the floor. Again none of the sleepers moved.

With an unfamiliar feeling of daring, John walked to the door and out into the passage. It led past the duty-men's room to the kitchen. Halfway along it the light on the wall-bracket glowed enough to show that the upper half of the door to the duty-men's room was ajar as always. John went to the door and tapped on it, loudly it sounded in the sleeping House.

He expected a movement from inside the room, and the half-door to be opened wider; but no sound answered his knock. He felt a trace of surprise that apparently no duty-man was awake through the night. After a few moments of uncertainty, he lifted his hand to knock again; but, instead, he pushed the half-door so that it swung wider. The light from the lamp in the passage showed two figures, blanket-wrapped, asleep on low beds. John stared at them, expecting that they would stir to ask him what he wanted; but the steady breathing persisted.

Still feeling unusually daring, John went on to the

kitchen. He hesitated at the closed door. Though he scarcely realised it, he had never been alone in the kitchen; always when sent to peel potatoes or prepare vegetables, there had been another boy with him, and always a duty-man, usually Ben, working at the long, scrubbed table or at the sink under the window. Perhaps Ben would be there now, John thought; and, restraining a feeling that he ought not to go in, he risked turning the door-handle.

There was no one in the room. As John slowly opened the door wider, he became aware of pale light coming in at the window. He frowned with slight puzzlement as he recognised the moonlight. He had always associated it with wintertime for, through the longer days, all the boys were on their bunks before dusk thickened into night. With a sense of discovery, he realised that the moon shone at other seasons and that the light now made it possible for him to see his way around the kitchen.

He went to the pump near the sink. As usual a bucket stood to catch the drips from the spout. It was half-full of water now. John began scooping it up in his hands and then knelt to drink more easily.

The water, less cold than that from the stream, had not the slight sickliness of the meal-time beakers-full. Cool and all but tasteless, it eased his thirst. It seemed to bring a recollection of something the dark-haired girl had said; but she had spoken so hurriedly that he had missed much.

He had moved nearer the window, his eyes towards the orchard outside; but the sight did not at once penetrate his consciousness. Then, abruptly, he was aware of the stretch of moonlit grass set about with apple-trees and, at the end, currant and gooseberry bushes. Just as he took in the strangeness of the familiar orchard rendered unfamiliar by the pale moonlight and the deep shadows, a portion of darkness detached itself from among the fruit bushes, and shaped itself into a dog-like animal that trotted with apparent unconcern across the grass. It was, John knew, a fox; there was a picture of one in the book he chanted from at Lesson Time. But in the story the animal was said to be crafty and sly, and in John's mind it had become linked with the Lost Ones who, like the fox, lived furtively. Now his eyes caught the ease with which the animal moved, the unhurried purposefulness very different from the lumbering movements he had always associated with people and so, by transfer, with those animals said to have human characteristics. The reality of the fox, so far from the vague imaginings prompted by the story, seemed to link more with the two girls he had seen. If they were truly Lost Ones they were no more like the frightened, dejected runaways he had pictured than the fox resembled the furtive, half-human creature of the story.

A drowsy grunting from the duty-men's room snatched his thoughts and his staring eyes from the moonlit orchard. Realising how strangely he was behaving, he looked over his shoulder at the glimmer in the passage; he could hardly recall how he had come to be in the kitchen at such a time, and alone. At last, hearing no more, he crept out past the duty-men's room, and so to the Dormitory.

As he reached his bunk he found that he was trembling. Again he frowned as he tried to understand; except from cold, he had never before experienced such a sensation. It took an effort for him to steady himself enough to climb on to his bunk without disturbing sleeping James. Though he could scarcely recognise it, he was experiencing fear. Through the dull, plodding days that made up what he could recall of his life, he had never known such a feeling . . . nor, as at last he lay on his mattress, had he ever before known the relief from evading danger, though as yet he did not know the substance of his danger.

The fear ebbed slowly and another new feeling began to spread through him, a feeling of achievement mingled with new-found excitement. He had, he realised, done things such as he had never done before, or thought to do. He had crept about the House during a forbidden time, he had seen a fox, he had drunk the pump-water, and no one knew!

*   *   *   *   *

John awoke suddenly to find the other boys already dressing. He squirmed off his bunk so hurriedly that he bumped into James who, with usual slowness, was dragging on his tunic. 'What you doing?' James asked without any trace of annoyance or curiosity in his voice.

John pulled on his clothes, unaware that he was doing so less slowly than usual. He felt a twinge of surprise when, joining the line forming at the door, he saw that several boys who had awoken before him, were still only half-dressed. A few minutes later he was again slightly surprised at the slowness with which the boys filed into the Meal Room. He felt unusually hungry and, on the order to sit, he got into his place on the bench so quickly that James lumbered into him. Caught off balance, James jolted the table and knocked over John's beaker. As he took his place beside John, James stared dully at the water spreading over the board.

'It's all right,' John said. 'I'm not thirsty.'

Duty-man Peter came towards them, cloth in hand, a rare hint of sullenness on his face. 'I don't know,' he mumbled as he mopped up the water. 'It would serve you right if you went without your drink.'

'I don't mind,' said John. 'I'm not thirsty.'

The duty-man, in the act of wiping the board, turned his head to look at John. For a long moment the dull gaze held John's eyes, making him realise that he had never before spoken so casually to a duty-man.

At last Duty-man Peter turned away. Beginning on his porridge, John saw the man go to Duty-man Martin, speak to him, and the pair of them turned uneasy eyes towards him.

Breakfast ended, the boys stood up to file out. Duty-man Peter beckoned to John. 'Go to the room,' he said.

John went to the duty-man's room. Though Peter had spoken in his usual flat voice, John wondered if the man could have come to know that he had walked about the House during the night, had been into the kitchen. A few times he had seen the duty-men doing inexplicable things that suggested they had powers beyond any John knew. In the duty-men's room there was an oddly shaped instrument into which John had seen a duty-man speaking as if, by some mysterious means, he was holding a conversation with someone not present; and more than once he had been puzzled when a duty-man, by putting a finger to a little knob on the wall, had set off a ringing about the House so that another duty-man had come to the room. And from snatches of conversation between duty-men he had gathered that, by some means quite beyond his understanding, the van-loads of black coal caused the vans to move about. The duty-men seemed able to guess what was to happen sometimes, too; John could recall occasions when all the boys had been set to cleaning the House – as if the duty-men had known that, within an hour or so, a Sub-Leader would be visiting. Recollection of such mysterious powers added to John's uneasiness as he reached the door to the duty-men's room.

Duty-man Martin opened the half-door to his knock. For a few moments he looked down at John as if not knowing why he should have come. 'Duty-man Peter sent me,' said John, and heard in his own voice a trace of irritation at the man's slowness.

'Are you all right?' Duty-man Martin asked him.

'Yes,' said John; and added: 'I don't feel sick or anything.'

The duty-man continued to regard him. 'I thought yesterday you weren't yourself. I thought the sun might have upset you.'

'I was all right.' Again John heard his own impatience. Never before had he noticed how ponderously the duty-men spoke.

'You'd best not go to the field today,' said Duty-man Martin. 'You'd best stay in the House.' He turned his head to look out of the window. 'It looks like being hot again.'

'I'm all right,' John persisted. 'It wasn't the sun. It was –'

He stopped as his mind, seeming to act with unaccustomed speed, caught the danger in telling of what had happened yesterday.

Duty-man Martin turned back to him. 'You can help Ben in the kitchen,' he said. 'We don't want you going sick, do we?'

Again, unnaturally it felt, John checked himself. The strangeness within himself, the awareness that he was thinking and speaking more quickly than he had done before, strengthened his uneasiness. If he said too much, if the lumbering, slow-thinking duty-man should realise that he had changed and, suspecting sickness, send for Matron. . .

Until then, John had not consciously felt any fear of Matron. He could remember little of her occasional visits to the House: seeing her drive up to the House door in her van which, though smaller than the vans that brought the supplies, seemed always to move more urgently, the smoke puffing importantly out of its tall funnel; and then the heavy bulk of the woman striding from Dormitory door to the bunk where a boy lay unwell. Until then, John had accepted that sickness or injury brought her. He had not before realised how rarely he had seen again the boy for whom Matron had been summoned. Always the boy had gone away with her – once John had seen a duty-man carrying a boy out to Matron's van – but only Howard could he remember returning. Howard had cut his leg falling on a spade; he had come back to the House the same day, his leg bandaged but otherwise unchanged. But Gregory who had awoken early – had it been months or years ago? – crying out in pain and holding his stomach: he had not come back. Nor had Edwin and that other boy who within an hour of each other had whimpered and shivered on their bunks. And Dennis whose face had become curiously blotched. . . had his name been Dennis?

'You go along to the kitchen for today.' Duty-man Martin's dull voice interrupted John's growing uneasiness. 'You'll be out of the sun there.'

John went, his brows unusually drawn down in a frown. Again, as several times during the past twenty-four hours, he felt aware of more than the surface of his immediate surroundings. Below that surface lurked disturbing ignorance; and, recalling as he neared the kitchen door how he had gone there and seen the fox in the moonlight, he felt there lurked undreamed-of possibilities, too.

Duty-man Ben was in the kitchen. He turned an expressionless face to John as he told that he had been sent to help. 'By yourself?' asked the duty-man; but, as if he had not expected an answer, he turned away, saying: 'You'd best start on the potatoes, then.'

The bucket under the pump's spout was already full of potatoes. John guessed that Duty-man Ben had been about to add water preparatory to peeling the potatoes. He pumped a few times and then, seeing the water gushing out, his eyes sharpened.

His mind seemed to be searching for a word the dark-haired girl had used about the water, but she had spoken so quickly. Only a fragment of her speech lingered, a phrase about the duty-men putting into the water something 'to keep you quiet'. John looked over his shoulder. Duty-man Ben was at the sink. John recalled drinking the pump water in the night; and at breakfast Duty-man Peter had been so caught by John's casual tone about spilling his beaker that he had forgotten to refill it. John looked again to make sure that Ben was not watching; then he bent down and gulped a mouthful from the bucket. It had an earthy taste from the potatoes, not the usual sickliness.

For an hour John squatted, peeling potatoes. Never had he realised how tedious a job it was. As he worked he found himself looking often at Duty-man Ben, and seeing with unusual clarity the man's face. Always before the duty-men had looked almost indistinguishable, each face wearing the same near-blank expression, each having the same dull gaze, each with the same unlined skin. But Ben, John now saw, was older than the other duty-men. His hair had a greyness John had not noticed before, the skin had a leathery texture, the nose was pinched.

As Ben turned to meet his look, John ventured: 'Did you live here when you were a boy?'

The man's gaze became fixed on John's face. 'What's that?' he asked in so dull a voice that it was hardly a question.

'I said: did you live here when you were a boy?'

'No. No, I didn't.' A trace of uncertainty in the dull tone hinted that the man could not remember. The duty-man went on: 'You'd best not ask about such things. It was a long time ago, and much happened that's best forgotten.'

'Have you forgotten it?' John asked, and then held himself a little stiffly, aware that he had spoken with a curiosity he had never felt before.

Again Duty-man Ben looked long at him. John saw the pale blue unblinking eyes, their stare blank but for a glimmer of suspicion. 'Are you all right?'

John had to keep his voice slow. 'Yes,' he said. 'I'm all right.'

At last the duty-man turned away, shaking his grey head. 'I don't know,' he muttered. 'Asking questions. Don't know what it'll lead to.'

* * * * *

Again that night sleep did not come easily to John. Again he lay staring into the gloom, hearing the even breathing of the other boys. But it was not thirst which kept him awake; four times as he had worked in the kitchen he had gulped a drink behind Duty-man Ben's back. At the evening Meal he had, with new-found cunning, waited until James had drunk his water and then, when the duty-men were not looking his way, had poured his water into James's beaker. James had drunk it as if unaware that he had already had his own beakerful.

Again and again during that day in the kitchen John had recalled the two girls. Much of what they had said still eluded him; but he had remembered more clearly the dark-haired girl with the quick, bright smile telling that the duty-men put something – John could not recall the word – into the drinking water and that it 'kept him quiet'. He remembered, too, the girl's impatience with the way he had repeated what she said; it matched the feeling that had since come to him whenever he had spoken to one of the duty-men. And somehow the girl had linked the water with the numbers nineteen ninety-seven, the numbers the District Party Leader had used at Celebrations and that seemed, oddly, to hint of a time.

That thought brought back his conversation with Duty-man Ben, and his realisation that the man was older than the other duty-men. Could it be, John wondered, that Ben had known of the time those numbers implied? Could it be that when he had spoken of a 'long time ago', he had meant nineteen ninety-seven? And, if that was so, why had he spoken of it being better to forget that time?

Staring up into the darkness, John realised that beyond his new-found awareness there stretched expanses of knowledge about which he knew nothing. He had grown up confined within the House and its immediate surroundings, his experience limited to the round of working and eating and sleeping, a seemingly endless sequence of days broken so rarely by a Celebration that such an event seemed an unreal intrusion, not a glimpse of another way of living. He did not even know what lay beyond the House and the few familiar fields about it, and the fragmentary roadway leading to the Local Centre; not until yesterday had he ventured beyond a known fence, and then only for a few, unexpectedly hurried paces. What had been beyond the stream where he had seen the two girls? Where did they live? Were there only the two of them, or could they be two of a group of people who lived somehow utterly differently from the life he had accepted as normal? He recalled the Local Party Centre as the only place he knew beyond his House, and a dim recollection of the Mothers'

House where he had lived for the first few years of his life. Did those girls live in such a place, and live there more alertly than he had ever done? Did they spend their time dancing about as he and the others had been allowed to do briefly at a Celebration? Could they possibly live without duty-men and duty-women telling them – and in such dull, heavy voices! – what was to be done, when to work, when to read, when to go to their bunks?

The questions crowded in on him, each new one seeming to start a dozen others. The first light of a new day was thinning the darkness that wrapped the Dormitory before, at last, John's thinking blurred from tiredness and he fell asleep.

* * * * *

For the second time John awoke unusually suddenly. Duty-man Peter was standing by his bunk looking at him.

John stared up into the dull eyes, aware again of the new feeling of fear. The thoughts that had come to him during the night rose up in his mind. Had he really lain awake thinking such strange ideas or had he merely dreamed them? And then he remembered the previous night and his wandering about the sleeping House and seeing the fox; and beyond that, his meeting with the two girls. Surely he had not dreamed them, too?

He became aware of the boys standing about the Dormitory, their eyes turned to him but showing no surprise that he, unlike them, was still on his bunk.

'Are you all right, John?' The duty-man's question recalled Duty-man Martin's when – had it been only two days ago? – he had struggled up from the stream of strange water.

John jerked up on the mattress. 'Yes, I'm all right,' he said with an unfamiliar sharpness, and then caught the uneasiness in the duty-man's eyes.

Duty-man Martin's voice, all but indistinguishable from Peter's, came from a slight distance along the Dormitory. 'It can't have been the sun the other day. We're getting Matron.'

At that John began to scramble from his bunk. 'No, not Matron!' His alarm gave his voice a tone he himself had never heard in it before.

Duty-man Peter laid a heavy hand on his shoulder. 'Now, don't excite yourself. There's nothing to worry about. Matron will soon put you right.'

'But I am all right! I – I feel –'

'Take it easy, John. Matron will know what to do.'

The man's hand was holding him, its grip not so much tight as restraining. To John as he squirmed to free himself, that hand seemed the embodiment of the restriction on his living, the firm, unthinking hold on his every action, his every thought.

'Just lie quiet.' The duty-man's dull, unfeeling tone sharpened John's alarm. 'Matron won't be long.'

At that John struggled afresh. 'Not Matron!' he cried again. Recollection of Gregory and Edwin and Dennis surged up again from the depths of his memory. 'What about the others? What happened to Dennis and – and Gregory? And Edwin? They didn't come back –!'

The duty-man's face, only a foot from his own, showed no glimmer of understanding. His grip on John's shoulder did not tighten, but the hand felt heavier. 'There's nothing to worry about, John. Matron will be here any minute.'

John stared into the impassive face. That Matron could come so soon – it was only minutes since he had awoken – seemed to give her a power that, until then, he had not realised. By some superhuman means the duty-men had already conveyed to her that he was unwell, had summoned her. His fear mounting afresh, he tried to struggle out of Duty-man Peter's hold, and his wild eyes, turning away from the vaguely watching faces of the other boys, caught the open window only a pace from his bunk. But so foreign to him was the idea of escape that the sight did not at once awaken a response. He continued to struggle, thoughtlessly, scarcely hearing the duty-man's attempts at reassurance until a clanking noise from outside snatched his attention. He heard the van crunching to a halt, the steam hissing out from underneath as the smoke's puffing eased; and then, moments later, Matron was striding through the Dormitory door. Only then did the duty-man's hand relax.

'All right. I'll deal with him.' Matron's voice had a sharp heaviness.

Staring as he squirmed back to his bunk's head, John saw that Matron's full face appeared to match her voice. The eyes were hard and quick, and the little mouth was compressed into a line.

'Now, boy, there's nothing to be afraid of!' Placing a leather box on the end of his bunk, she demanded: 'What have you been up to?'

'Nothing!'

'Have you been eating anything you've been told not to? Have you drunk any water?'

John stared. In his unnaturally quickened mind he heard the dark-haired girl's voice: 'that powder the duty-men put into the water. . . to keep you quiet.'

Matron's eyes became piercing. 'Well, have you? Have you been drinking at the river?'

'No!' John clutched at the brittle truth. He could not have invented a direct lie. 'No, I haven't drunk at the river!'

Above his mounting alarm, John heard Duty-man Peter, half-hidden from him by Matron's bulk, telling her: 'He was funny the day before yesterday. Martin thought it might be the sun.'

'It's not that!' Matron sharply dismissed the possibility. She opened the leather box and began to search in it. 'It's more likely that he's becoming resistant,' she added.

'Resistant?' echoed Duty-man Peter and for once John caught a trace of feeling in the man's dull tone. It told that John had done something utterly unforgivable.

'We get cases from time to time,' Matron said, 'since the Party replaced those long-acting drugs with these new ones. Why they should have given up the old ones, I don't know.

They don't ask those of us who have to do the work what we think!'

She had taken from the box a tube-like instrument ending in a long, sharp point. As John stared, his alarm growing ever stronger, she stuck the point into a little bottle she held in her other hand. 'Roll up your sleeve!' she commanded.

Her sharp, indisputable tone, contrasting with the dull, heavy voices he had known for so long, increased John's fear beyond restraining. For a moment he continued to stare at her free hand reaching towards him, the tube-like pointed thing raised in the other hand. He saw, too, that Duty-man Peter was still standing a few paces behind her; and, as he turned desperately away, he saw again that the nearby window was open.

John squirmed from her, half-scrambling, half-falling from the bunk. He heard Matron gasp: 'Stop him!' but he had flung himself towards the window before the duty-man had moved, was swinging himself over the sill so that he dropped on his feet outside. The next instant he was running. He did not know why or where; he knew only that he was able to run faster than he had ever known he could.

3

Escape

OUTSIDE the window, John urged himself towards the only way of escape he knew: the break in the fence at the far end of the potato-field.

Early morning mistiness still hung along the riverside, but so familiar was the way that it did not impede him; nor did he see that already the rising sun was bringing a glow to the mist, foretelling that soon the slight protection would disperse. He ran on and on, heedless; not until the fence was only a few paces ahead did he flash a fearful glance over his shoulder. The misty blankness that met his eyes brought a momentary feeling of relief; but he could hear heavy feet lumbering after him – how far behind he could not guess – and into the quiet air rose the urgent puffing of Matron's van as it started up the hill from his House.

He had reached the fence a dozen paces from the gap through which he had fallen. For a few fearful moments he stared along the fence, his eyes searching desperately, his ears catching the duty-men's ponderous footsteps; then, sighting the gap, he forced himself through it. He managed to keep his footing on the slope down to the stream, splashed across it and struggled up the other side. Thorny branches clutched at him, bramble-fronds all but snared him; but his feet seemed of themselves to take an easy way through the thicket until a great sweep of bramble brought him, panting, to a stop.

Never before had he known that he could run so far and so fast; but the feeling of achievement was snatched away by the sounds of the duty-men crashing through the growth behind him. Over the higher brambles he glimpsed ahead a field sweeping up through the thinning mist. At the sight he struggled out of the brambles, forced his way around them, pushed through a hawthorn bush. On the field's expanse he would again be able to run.

He was out in the open, running up past cows that turned to look solemnly surprised, when the sunlight striking through the last wraiths of mist showed ahead a group of buildings which he guessed must be another House. Instinctively he slowed; and then saw Matron's van passing the House and turning as if to cross the field ahead of him. In its box-like rear portion were two more duty-men.

John could not reason that Matron was moving to cut off his way of escape. He knew only his fear and that behind him the duty-men from his House were crashing through the bushes he had just left. Without thinking, he had turned aside and was dashing for the growth, still mist-wrapped, along the river. The ground's tilt helped him until he was staggering among rushes, and dark mud was sucking at his feet.

He was panting heavily, his heart was pounding, and his legs were shaking from the unaccustomed exertion. Ahead he saw the river sliding by, the fearsome river of the story. Behind him more crashing sounds told that his pursuers knew in which direction he had gone. He caught Matron's sharp command: 'Spread out! He can't be far!'

Such was his fear that John saw only the river's danger, not that it was barely a dozen paces to the far bank now visible through the thinning mist. The thrusting, crashing sounds of the duty-men seemed to be converging on him. At any moment one of them would see him crouching at the water's edge, would come to seize him, to drag him back. And then. . .

That he could not even guess what might happen to him sharpened John's fear still more. He knew only that Eric's disappearance had brought concern to the duty-men's faces and the sharp-eyed District Party Leader to the

House. The other boys whom Matron had taken away had vanished into a fear-filled nothingness. As the clumsy footsteps came ever nearer, John forced himself in desperation towards the water –

'Go on! It's not deep!'

The girl's call from across the river cut through John's fear, checked the despair that was all but overwhelming him.

'Quick! They're coming!'

John heard a shout behind him and knew that he had been seen. He flung himself towards where the girl sounded to be, floundering into the water, forcing himself through its sudden chill. Only vaguely was he aware that his feet still found firmness until, sliding into a hole in the bottom, he all but fell. As he threshed his arms about, the water seemed by some inexplicable means to hold him up; and then he was struggling out of the river. Unbelievably he had crossed the danger and, as unbelievably, the river had done him no harm.

'Quick! Keep down – and run!'

He caught sight of the girl, a face framed with dark hair among the ivy straggling over a bush; and then she was off, crouching as she ran. As John began to follow, a duty-man's shout told that he had been seen. John forced himself to run faster, compelled his shaking legs to keep him within sight of the girl's darting course around bramble clumps and thorn thickets.

And then, suddenly, she was not ahead of him. As John staggered to a panting halt, he heard Matron's voice: 'You'll have to get across, too, then!'

A fierce whisper, only a pace from John, seemed to answer Matron. 'In here, quick!' He swung towards the sound, saw what had been a building all but hidden under a great clambering of ivy. At a gap in a wall, he glimpsed the girl's face pale against the darkness inside. 'Come on!' she urged.

Ivy all but filled the holes that had been windows; more

plants had taken root in the rotted floor so that, inside, the green darkness was baffling. John saw that the girl was climbing through a window on the far side. 'They're only just behind!' she whispered urgently.

He struggled after her into the tangle of ivy and bushes outside. The girl caught his arm. 'Now, keep down – and keep still!'

Panting and bewildered by the unfamiliar idea of hiding, John crouched beside her. Though he realised that thick growth would mask them from outside the building, he was aware that the window gap through which he had scrambled was a mere pace away. Hearing heavy steps approaching, he started, and at once the girl's hand tightened on his arm. He stared at her as the footsteps came nearer, scarcely seeing through his fear that her dark eyes were lit with cunning.

'I'd better look inside.' The familiar dullness of a duty-man's voice sounded only yards away; and the next moment John heard him struggling into the building and grunting as he moved about the broken, growth-tangled floor. Had not the girl's grasp held tight, John's fear would have forced him to jump up, to run. . .

The sounds from within the building receded. 'Someone's been in there,' came a duty-man's voice.

'Could it be him?' asked another, the tone as always heavy and incurious.

'No. There's nowhere for him to be hiding. It must have been some Lost One.'

John looked at the girl and met her quick smile. But he saw, too, that she was still listening to the sounds of the duty-men moving on with their search. Vaguely John realised that the hiding-place she had chosen among the growth surrounding the building had been safer than the more obvious refuge of the place itself.

After what seemed to him several long moments, the girl whispered: 'We'll risk it. And keep quiet. I heard you a mile away!'

John stared, not understanding. 'But they've gone –'

'They'll be back when they don't find you along there. Come on, but don't go crashing about, and look where you put your feet. Don't tread on any dry twigs!' Catching John's bewilderment, she added: 'They snap when you tread on them. . . and I mustn't forget the eggs.'

She picked up a little cloth-wrapped packet, climbed back into the building, and slipped soundlessly through the tangle inside. At what had been the door, she paused to listen again. Following, John became aware of his own clumsiness.

She nodded towards the ground rising up away from the river, the bushes and trees on it now cleared of mist. 'There's a good hide up there,' she whispered. 'Go quietly and keep down. Near the top there's a beech-tree and after that –' The girl checked herself at John's puzzlement, and the impatience faded from her eyes. 'I suppose I didn't know what a beech-tree was a few months ago,' she whispered. 'The bark's light, silvery almost. It stands by itself near the top. I'll be there.'

At once she was off. John stared as she disappeared into the growth that reached up from the river-bank; and then, catching again the sounds of the duty-men along the riverside, he scurried to the shelter of the nearest hawthorn. He thought he saw the girl ahead; as he struggled upwards, he recalled her warning about dry twigs and tried to keep his eyes on the ground. He did not notice that the growth was thinning until he was approaching the top of the rise. A few scant thorn-bushes, beyond them a solitary pale-trunked tree. . . there was no sign of the girl.

John knew that he had to cross the openness around that tree. He expected to hear at any moment a duty-man's shout from below, the crashing pursuit resumed; but he crept on, head lowered, towards the tree that stood so exposed. . .

'You did that quite well.'

John stared. He had seen nothing of the girl until she

spoke. She was lying at the tree's foot between two massive, clutching roots. 'You kept below the skyline,' she added approvingly. 'Get down – and mind my eggs!'

She snatched up the cloth-wrapped packet as John dropped beside her. 'That's why I was down by the river so late,' she added as if in explanation. 'Look! Four of them!' She unwrapped the cloth and John saw four eggs, unexpectedly pale blue. 'There's a lot of duck along the river,' the girl said, 'but it's risky to go there in the dark.'

So much had happened to John since he had awoken that morning that he felt dazed, and the girl's quick flinging out of ideas that were utterly new to him added to his confusion. He had to snatch at phrases in her quick speech, to try and shape them into some kind of sense. Vaguely he assumed that eggs of such unusual blueness must be connected with her being near the river.

She raised her head to look towards the open ground spreading beyond the tree. 'We can hide out there until it's dark,' she said.

John expected her to move at once, to go dashing off again. . . and then he became aware that she was listening. He could not hear any sounds from the riverside. As he looked questioningly at her, he realised that she was more concerned with the way ahead. After several long seconds, she said: 'I think the patrol must have passed by now.'

'The patrol?' John repeated.

She nodded. 'They use a lane over there. They go fairly regularly usually, though today may not be usual for them!' She gave a quick smile, but John did not link her words with himself. He was wondering what a patrol might be. She went on: 'There's a hollow out there. We'll have to run for it. I'll go first. If you hear them shout or anything, don't follow. All right?'

Questions, only half-formed, were rising to John's lips; but she spoke so hurriedly, hinted of so much that was new to him, that he could not find words before she was off.

John saw her run, crouching, to the rim of the hillside, and disappear over it. Several moments later he recalled her warning, but no sounds from along the river had responded to her going. He began crawling after her. Beyond the beech-tree he felt alarmingly exposed. Ahead the hillside, bare except for a few random thorn-bushes, rose towards an empty skyline that might screen unguessed dangers. And then, recalling how the girl had gone, John jumped up and, bending, ran towards where she had disappeared.

Coming over the rim of the slope he saw ahead only a wide empty field, its expanse broken by a few tufts of taller grass and clusters of what might be nettles. The far side was fully twice the potato field's length away, too far for the girl to have reached even at her speed; and yet again she had vanished.

Alarmed astonishment almost stopped him. Still crouching, John had to urge himself onwards, feeling more conspicuous with every step; feeling, too, amazement at the girl. At one moment her dark eyes were smiling easily, then with a gabble of instructions she was utterly gone. And she had, incredibly, led him out into a shelterless field which seemed to spread wider and wider as he ran. He expected shouting to break out behind him, footsteps to come thudding –

'Here!'

Again her call startled him by its nearness; and then he saw her lying on the bare, open grass only a pace or two away.

'Get down quick!'

John flung himself beside her. He lay panting but still feeling the emptiness of the field all about him. Inexplicably, the girl's eyes were again lit with triumphant cunning. 'We've done it!'

John could not understand. She had spoken of hiding – and until night, too! – and they were lying out in the middle of a huge field without a twig of bramble or a single thorn-bush to screen them.

'No – don't look up!'

John dropped flat again, utterly bewildered. He dared not look at the girl until she said in an easy voice that at first added to his alarm: 'If we keep down, the patrol won't see us. All they'd see is what looks like an empty field without anywhere to hide. . . unless they got out of their van and walked right up to us, and that isn't likely.'

John continued to stare until the telling phrases in her quick talk penetrated. 'Patrol' must be her word for dutymen; and he and the girl were lying in a shallow hollow that seemed so open and yet had kept her hidden until he had almost reached her. From deep in his memory he suddenly recalled the sight of a brown bird crouching on its nest in the grass fringing a field in which he had been working; he had all but trodden on it before he had seen it. At the time the sight had seemed of no significance; now he realised that even so slight a hollow as that in which they were lying could, if they kept still, provide safer hiding than a more obvious thicket.

He stared at her in admiration, and was amazed that she seemed able to read his thoughts. 'I couldn't understand at first. I just dashed to the nearest clump of trees, and they hadn't any leaves – it was January! I didn't know about patrols or anything like that. If Eric hadn't spotted me – Why, you're still wearing your night tunic!'

'Eh?' Her abrupt change of subject, seeming part of her quick brightness, baffled him afresh. 'I – I'd only just woken up. . . and Matron came and –'

'Have you had any breakfast?' And then, before he could reply: 'Neither had I when I ran away. I've learnt since then!'

The girl pulled out of her trews' pocket what looked to John like a misshapen oat-cake. 'It's potato and bean mostly,' she said, 'and we're low on fat.' She held it out to him. 'It'll help you to last out.' As John took it, she added: 'We'll get thirsty, too, if we're here all day.'

Incomprehensibly, she began digging with her fingers into the ground on which they lay. Catching John's stare, she appeared to associate it with the soft sandiness of the earth. 'Duncan thinks it's something to do with a game they played with a ball and a stick back in nineteen ninety-seven. . . Here's one!'

John expected her to pull a ball or a stick out of the ground but, even more surprising, she drew up a bottle. Again she smiled at his astonishment. 'We hide them in case,' she explained. 'When Helen and I saw you the other day at the spring, we'd just been refilling it.' She held out the bottle to him. 'It's only water, and it's not doped.'

John recalled the phrase and, as he tasted the cool, earthy water he realised that not for three days had he drunk from his meal-time beaker, and during those three days a bewildering change had come over him. It was as if he had woken from sleep not to the usual plodding work, but to a multitude of new experiences and – strangest of all – to an awareness of himself.

The realisation brought more new ideas surging up into his mind; but before he could frame them into words, into questions the girl might be able to answer, she turned his thoughts aside by warning him: 'Don't drink too much. It may have to last us all day.'

She pushed the bottle back into the ground. 'We'll have to refill it at the spring when we can,' she went on; and then, with another of her abrupt changes of talk: 'It's going to be hot lying here. Take off your tunic.'

John stared uncomprehending as she squirmed out of her own tunic. He glimpsed scratches on her back and guessed that they must have been made by brambles. 'Stuff your tunic with grass,' she told him. 'It'll keep the sun off.' She began pulling at the tufts around them, thrusting the grass into her tunic. 'And feel for sticks to prop it up,' she added.

By the time John had dragged off his tunic and filled it with grass, she had made hers into a kind of shelter, propped up a few inches above her face. 'It's better than lying in the sun all day,' she said. When he had poised his own grass-plumped tunic above him, she smiled and added:

'You got the idea quickly, considering. . . You can go to sleep if you like. It's hours before it'll be dark enough.'

After the confusion of happenings that had followed his escape through the Dormitory window, John found her suggestion of sleeping as incomprehensible as all the other new ideas she had flung at him. He lay staring up at his night-tunic, trying to understand all that had happened, trying to find meanings in her quickly spoken words. Something she had said – it had been just after he had run to the hollow where they now were – was trying to make itself understood, something about when she had run away. . . but he couldn't recall what it had been.

The girl was looking at him. 'What is it?' she asked. 'Are you wishing you hadn't run away?'

'No!' His reply came so quickly that it surprised him. It had not arisen from any conscious thoughts about the House and the duty-men and Matron, or from the driving fear which had sent him scrambling through the window. His unnaturally quick answer had been forced out by feelings that had come to him through the past hour, the sudden awareness that he was able to run, that he could experience the exhilaration of escaping, that he could triumph over the river's danger. Never before had he experienced such feelings.

'You're sure?' the girl persisted, her tone hinting that she might be disappointed if he was uncertain – and that was another discovery for him. His own voice took on an unfamiliar decisiveness: 'I'm quite sure. I – I couldn't go back, not now!'

She smiled quickly, as if she had achieved something. 'This is only the third time I've been out on my own – as far as this, anyway. Always Helen's been with me: she's been my trainer. And I've found a new runaway!'

John felt her delight though he could not understand what prompted it.

Her brightness wavered a little. 'You want to join us, don't you?'

Again he was puzzled. 'You mean there are more than

that other girl – the one who was with you the other day?'

'Oh yes! I mustn't tell you all of it; I couldn't anyway because I don't understand it all and I was voted in only a few weeks ago. But there are others of us; and we. . .' She hesitated as if she feared saying too much. 'We're all runaways – that means we're against the Party and the way they make everyone work for them and dope the water. But that's only the beginning of it. I can't tell you about it, but you'll come to learn. . . that is, if Eric and the others agree that you can join –'

'Eric?' John caught at the name. She had spoken of Eric before – it was the idea that he had been trying to recall – but her quick speech had made him pass it by.

The girl understood before his question was clearly formed. 'Did you say – the other day when Helen and I saw you – that you lived in Watford?'

Again her abrupt change of conversation was confusing him. 'I – I'm Watford Nine John. I don't know –'

'Eric came from Watford! He may remember you. If he does, it'll be all right when we have to vote on you!'

John could catch only part of her meaning. The Eric of whom she was speaking must be the boy who – had it been two or three years ago? – had disappeared, had caused such uneasiness among the duty-men, and had brought the sharp-eyed, thin-faced District Party Leader to the House.

The girl went on in an excited whisper different from any voice he had ever heard: 'I hope Eric will let me be your trainer; he probably will, as we're the same age. . . You'll have to have a trainer for a while, to help you find your way about and to show you where to work and how to hide and – and so on. I'm sure Eric will let me as I found you! And then, when the time comes, I won't have to go with Hugh!'

Though he could only guess at part of her meaning, John felt himself responding to her quick hopefulness. Never before had he met with such ease of expression. The only relief he had known from the dull, heavy atmosphere of the House – the crude attempts at jollity at a Celebration – seemed suddenly unreal and meaningless. To think that she – and others, too! – lived able to speak quickly, to voice their feelings, to share their thoughts –

'Eh?' He became aware that she had spoken again.

'I said we don't use places and numbers with our names. We'll call you just John. I'm Janet, so we're the same year. I came from Tring, but I've almost forgotten all about that. We all use just the one name. Eric says it's not where we've come from that matters but where we're going to.'

Janet: John liked the crispness of the name. It suited her.

* * * * *

Some time during the warm, almost summer-heavy afternoon, John dozed. Afterwards, he felt it incredible that he could have done; but one moment he had been dreaming of forcing himself through an interminable bramble-thicket before suddenly wading across a swirling river. . . and then a hand was shaking him and he was staring up at a kind of thick cloud, dull blue like his tunic, poised above his face.

'It's time,' Janet said in a low voice.

John stared at her, realising that it had not all been a dream. Her tunic on again, she was holding out a potato-and-bean cake to him and smiling at his sleepiness. 'Here. . . and I've left a mouthful of water.'

She moved his tunic aside and pulled out its grassy filling. 'We mustn't leave anything to show that we've been here,' she said, spreading the grass.

Recollection was streaming back, but as he ate there lingered in John's mind a feeling of unreality, so strange was it to find himself out of the House, under a darkening sky, and in a wide field about which seemed to stretch huge possibilities. He felt he wanted to jump up, to run, to shout, to fling himself into his sudden freedom. . . but, catching Janet's amused look, he recalled that but for her he would surely have blundered into a duty-man, and that there must be unknown dangers ahead.

She thrust the bottle into its hiding-place, and smoothed the earth over it. 'Ready?' she asked. 'Come on, then.'

Still scarcely able to believe what had happened, John followed as at first she returned to the cover of the growth reaching up from the river, then kept to a low hedge around a field, then along the fringe of a wood. There was still enough light to guide them though John found his legs had become unusually stiff and he stumbled on unevennesses of the ground or blundered into out-reaching branches. Struggling to keep up with her, he was struck by her quick, unfaltering, purposeful walk, and was reminded of the fox he had seen in the moonlit orchard.

Then, abruptly, they came to a steep slope down to a roadway far wider than any John had seen. Janet paused, peering along its empty reach. 'You never know if a patrol might come,' she whispered. 'They don't often because it's blocked along there where the bridge was.'

Following her glance, John made out that perhaps a hundred paces along the roadway it appeared to end at a confusion of massive lumps of stone out of which bushes were growing; it was as if another, lesser roadway had crossed the wide one, but had long ago been smashed down to form a barrier.

Apparently satisfied that there was no danger, Janet led down the slope. At the bottom, near a clump of bushes that had found rooting at a break in the smooth surface of the roadway, she stopped again to listen; and then, with a nod to John to follow, she ran to the far side and scrambled up to the safety of a copse.

Across two fields they struck another, narrower roadway, its surface broken where long ago tufts of weed or a few saplings had pushed through. As if thinking John might be surprised that she took so defined a route, Janet said in a low voice: 'This lane leads to the bridge. They don't patrol it.' John supposed that 'the bridge' must have been where the lane had crossed the wide roadway.

After a while the lane joined another, clearer one. 'Keep near the hedge,' Janet whispered, and John guessed that the lane was in use. Some minutes later he heard, distantly, the rumble of a duty-man's van. He looked quickly at Janet but her face showed no alarm. 'Into the field,' she whispered. 'Here's a place we can get through the hedge.' She pushed through into what looked like a grain-field. As John joined her, she added: 'Get down. Choose a place where there aren't nettles or brambles. And don't move!'

In a moment she was lying flat just within the hedge. John dropped beside her and, though his face found a tuft of weed and a prickly twig caught his sleeve, he held himself still. Before the van's lights were visible through the hedge, he had a few moments to appreciate the skill with which Janet evaded notice. The duty-men – John had no doubt that the van carried duty-men – would be looking for a figure running away across the open field or darting for cover among the darkening trees; they would not expect him to be hiding only a pace or two from the roadway.

They lay still until the van had rumbled well beyond them. Then, Janet leading, they went on alongside the hedge. The moon began to glint through the treetops ahead, helping John around another field and along the edge of a wood to where a roofless building loomed from behind thickly straggling bushes. 'Would you like another drink?' Janet asked abruptly.

John was both hungry and thirsty; he was tired, too, but he did not say so.

Janet led along what had been a path around the building, and then climbed in a hole in the wall that had once been a window. 'Careful,' she whispered. 'The floor's rotten.'

Scrambling in after her, John managed to find firm footing. Janet was almost immersed in the blackness. She sounded to be opening a door, and a moment later she was offering him a bottle. 'You can have half,' she whispered.

'That's another we must remember to refill.'

Again as he tasted the water, John recalled the change that had come to him during the past few days. He ventured: 'The water that the duty-men give us: you said it was different. . .?'

Her warning look told him to keep his voice down. 'It's doped. I told you. . . but you weren't able to understand then.'

With a new feeling of curiosity John asked: 'What is "doped"? Does it make me feel – different somehow?'

'No; it stops you feeling. That's the Party's idea – so that we can't feel properly awake. The duty-men and women put stuff in the water – called tranquillers or something. It's so that everyone goes on working. You'll come to understand.'

John frowned his puzzlement. He was looking towards the window-gap, but not until the girl said: 'That's one of our plots', did he notice that the moonlight outside showed unexpectedly a cleared space, perhaps thirty paces each way, on which were rows of sprouting plants as on the fields about his House.

'It looks as if the potatoes need earthing up,' she added. 'Perhaps we'll be doing it tomorrow.' She gave a light laugh. 'That'll be a change for you!'

For once she misread his surprise. 'What did you think we do for food?' she asked. 'Did you think we stole it?'

'I – I didn't think –'

'We don't steal, whatever happens! Eric says that if we can't live without stealing, there's no point in what we're doing. And we wouldn't be able to go –' She stopped herself as if she had been about to say more than she intended. 'Anyone who steals we would abandon,' she added.

'Abandon?'

'We'd take them to the Island and leave them there. If they couldn't get away and find a House, they'd starve. . . We'd better go on.'

John heard her return the bottle to a dark patch in the

wall; but when he went to follow her out of the window he again felt how stiff his legs had become. He had exerted himself far more that day than he had ever known he could. He had to whisper: 'Is it much farther?'

Janet did not reply as immediately as he had come to expect. Looking steadily at him, she said: 'I'll keep it as short as I can. I can't take you the quickest way – not until the others have agreed.' Catching John's puzzled frown, she added: 'If you don't know the way, you can't tell if you're caught.'

She led quickly round the plot. John had almost to run to follow as she turned in among the screening trees. Her going scarcely ruffled the twigs and branches that reached out to catch him. Behind another building they came out on to a space strewn with prickly bushes, and then, after groping through a thicket, he was passing more buildings. Though he had to hurry to keep up with the girl, John realised that many of the buildings were mere fragments of walls – once they crossed a space cluttered with fallen bricks – but others looked more nearly complete, their dark window-spaces staring blankly. Now and again Janet led across a roadway but did not again follow one. To John, panting after her, it seemed that always she chose hidden ways, moving with astonishing ease from one tree-screened darkness to another or going silently through the shadow of a wall or an overgrown hedge.

She stopped so abruptly that John nearly bumped into her. He had only just seen her vanish into the deeper darkness under a tree towering almost black in the moonlight; and then he was beside her. 'Wait here!' she whispered. 'Don't move whatever happens. I'll be a few minutes.'

She slipped across a moon-silvered space and disappeared into a thicket of more dark bushes. John stared after her, trying to make out which way she was going; but he heard no sound until away to his left a bird fluttered. He wondered if she could have disturbed it.

He stood still, his eyes intent, his ears straining. He

caught whispers of sound in the growth about him. He nearly jumped at a sudden harsh cry almost overhead – but he recalled the owl's screech that he had heard of an evening in the House. The recognition brought thoughts of the other boys. They would now be sitting at the long table, their old tattered story-books before them. . . Or had they by now gone to their bunks?

Not for hours, not since he had awoken in that open yet unexpectedly secure hollow in the middle of the bare field, had he thought about the House and what might be happening there. Were duty-men still looking for him? Had a duty-man or Matron sent for the District Party Leader? Was the man even now walking briskly about the House, his eyes piercing, his voice sharp? Would he send out more duty-men to search? John recalled the girl's talk of 'patrols'; had she meant that already duty-men were in their vans seeking him? Clearly she – and Eric, too, and that fair girl who had been at the spring – must live always with the risk that a duty-man would see them, that they would be caught, and then. . .

His thoughts stumbled as again he reached the limit of his little knowledge. The stories had implied that such disobedience as the girl's and Eric's and the others' would be severely punished, but the form of punishment had been left vague. Never before had John thought of such a matter. His mind slipped to the day when Eric had disappeared. What would have happened if the duty-men had caught him? Would they have brought him back to the House and there. . . done what? Or would they have taken him to the Local Centre, or even to the District Leader? Or perhaps – John caught at the memory of a duty-man saying that Eric had been due to leave the House shortly, anyway – there were other places about which John had never heard?

Again he was sharply aware of how little he knew. What would have been ahead of him if he had stayed on at the House until he was of an age to leave? What happened to the boys who left the House? John could recall seeing them file away up the road, a duty-man walking beside them, but never had he heard where they went. Always they had, within a mere day or two, slipped out of his memory. . .

An unseen fly buzzing about his head brought him abruptly back to the moment. His arm wanted to respond to the fly's annoyance; but, recalling the girl's warning, he had held himself still. Or had the fears rising up in his mind checked him? To be caught, to be taken away by the duty-men. . . Again he felt an almost overwhelming sense of his own vulnerability, of being surrounded by a huge fear-filled ignorance.

His eyes were still fixed on the cluster of shadows among which Janet had disappeared. For how much longer would he have to wait while uncertainties brought new fears into his mind and the shadows seemed to be moving? And yet, even as his fears grew afresh, he recalled the girl, the easy way she spoke, the ready laugh, the brightness of her. How strange that she could look as she did, act so light-heartedly, if she too felt all about her unknown dangers –

John suddenly saw a figure standing only a few paces from him, a man with his face turned towards him. At once he assumed a duty-man. . . until he realised that no duty-man could have approached him so silently or would be standing utterly still. In the pale light, he could see the darkness of a beard and above it the hollows of the eyes.

The man's unseen gaze seemed to be reaching towards John as if urging him to show himself. But John again recalled Janet's warning; he remembered, too, the pair of them lying still behind the hedge as the van rumbled past, and the bird nesting on the ground at a field's edge. He understood the safety in stillness.

'Watford Nine John?'

The whisper crossed the space between the man and John. Then the man began to walk towards him. John caught a hint of familiarity about the shape of the head, a familiarity that had somehow changed.

The man stopped again only a pace or two away. 'It's all right, John. You've begun to learn already. I'd never have known you were there if Janet hadn't told me.'

The voice was not that which John had known. It had now a man's depth; it had, too, an expressiveness far beyond the dull tones of a boy at the House. Yet the shape of the head stirred John's memory. 'You – you're Watford Nine Eric!' he stammered.

'You've remembered me!' There was a laugh in the lowered voice. 'That's a good start. Come along in and meet the others.'

4

The Sudden Spring

NEVER in his thirteen years had John dreamed that life could be as he lived it during the next weeks. There was about it a vividness and a purposefulness such as he had never known. At first he had to keep reminding himself that the seven of them were what he had been taught to call Lost Ones, they were so unlike the hunted, dejected people of the story.

They lived in low-ceilinged rooms under what had been an old building. Eric had led him through a thicket of evergreen bushes and down a short flight of stone steps so hidden that John knew he would have passed it unnoticed even by daylight. He found himself in a room smaller than any in the House, blinking in the light from two flames reaching up from saucers of fat. Out of the shadows on the walls, faces looked towards him, smiling or inquisitive faces whose alertness made them appear utterly different from those gathered about the meal-table at the House. John could only stare open-mouthed, unable to take in Eric's quick introductions; and then one – in the yellow light John did not recognise the fair-haired girl whom he had seen at the spring with Janet – was offering him a plate on which were a few cakes of potato and bean. 'You look hungry,' she said with a smile.

John took a cake and then with a surge of relief recognised Janet. The light striking upwards had given her small features an unexpected appearance, but the smile dancing in her eyes were unmistakable.

Munching the cake, John scarcely understood what Eric meant as he spoke of his 'taking time to get used to the change'. Others spoke, but their words, uttered more speedily than John was used to, seemed unable to penetrate his suddenly weary mind. Eric's voice saying something about 'all that he must have been through since he left his House', seemed to come to him from an increasing distance as John felt exhaustion overwhelming him. The faces about him abruptly took on looks of concern, a round-faced bearded man started up from his seat, the protruding eyes of a girl with dangling hair seemed to be reaching across the table; and then John's vision blurred. . .

He was only dimly aware of Janet's cry, of Eric saying 'he's tired out', of an arm about his shoulders helping him towards a door he had not noticed. Then the darkness within another small room seemed to be rising up into his face until a light was causing shadows to jump about the walls before the fair-haired girl set it on a stool beside a mattress on the floor. 'You'll feel better when you've had a sleep,' she said as the red-bearded man helped John on to the mattress.

* * * * *

John opened his eyes to stare up at a blotched ceiling lit by a greenish light. He jerked up his head, fear starting –

'It's all right.'

Though the voice was easy, John turned sharply. The man with the thick red beard was squatting beside him. 'It's all right,' he said again. 'You're not dreaming. . . I'm Ewan, by the way. You won't remember from last night. It's always very confusing at first.'

As John's alarm ebbed, he recalled having seen the man before. But then he had not noticed the reassuring smile in the brown eyes. Ewan, he repeated to himself as if needing to associate a name with the feeling of ease that the man's appearance brought.

He became aware that on another mattress nearby someone else was sleeping. He saw a fair head, so pale that it was almost white, protruding out of neatly patched blankets.

'That's Hugh.' Ewan's smiling eyes had followed his look. 'You met him, too, last night. You'll soon get to know us. . . You'll be wanting the loo. I'll show you.'

As he got up, John saw that he was in a small room lit by a window just under the ceiling. Through the window he saw a cluster of weedy growth, and recalled Eric leading him down steps into the place.

'Eric?' he asked abruptly.

'He's about somewhere,' Ewan spoke casually. 'Come along. First things first.'

He led the way to a door that opened on to the flight of stone steps. Up a few steps, Ewan stopped to peer through a clump of brambles masking the entrance. 'It's all right.' His voice, though low, was still easy. 'You always have to take a look first. You never know when a patrol might be having a look around.'

He led along the wall of the building. Turning a corner John saw that little more than the single wall remained above-ground; behind it was a heap of fallen brickwork out of which weeds and saplings straggled. At a flimsy, bush-screened hut leaning against a fragment of wall, Ewan said: 'I'll wait to make sure you can find your way back.'

They returned not to the room where John had slept, but to the larger one to which Eric had first brought him. About the table four of them were sitting, Janet looking quickly at him, the fair-haired girl smiling, another man taller than Ewan and with a long, thin face, and the girl with lank hair. At first John did not see Eric; he was standing apart, apparently peering into a dark hole in the wall. He turned to give John a nod and then resumed looking into the hole.

'Food,' said Ewan. 'If John's as hungry as I am, he's ready for it,' As the fair girl turned to a small table in one corner, Ewan asked her: 'What is it today, Helen? More potato-and-bean cakes for a change?'

'No, it isn't!' John heard the fair girl's feigned indignation. 'Janet found some eggs yesterday.'

'Eggs and a new runaway!' Ewan smiled at Janet. 'Quite a morning's work for you!'

'I'd just found another nest when I saw John,' Janet told him. 'There must be several along the river.'

The tall, long-faced man smiled across the table. 'As John interrupted you, perhaps he doesn't deserve to have eggs.'

The quick, easy bantering was different from any way of talking that John had ever heard. He assumed that the tall man was serious; his surprised look as Helen put a plate of potato and scrambled egg before him made Ewan chuckle. 'You'll soon get used to us,' he said. 'Soon you'll be having to search for eggs so you'll make up for the ones Janet didn't get.'

Helen's full-cheeked smile wavered a little as she misread John's bewilderment. 'The food has to be cold,' she told him. 'We can't risk a fire during the day. The smoke might be seen.' Not until John had begun on the food did he understand what she meant.

'Any eggs left for me?' asked a voice from behind John, and he saw that the boy with near-white hair had joined them from the other room. As the boy took a seat at the table, John noticed a sharpness in the pale eyes, a look almost of suspicion. 'You're only – how old? Thirteen?' the boy asked him.

From by the hole in the wall Eric said: 'We've voted, Hugh. There's nothing more to be said.'

Eating hungrily, John heard the firmness in Eric's voice, and he saw a responding look of sullenness on the boy Hugh's pink face and in Janet's eyes something near to anger. But so unfamiliar were the expressions on the differing faces, and so quickly did they change, that John could not read them. He had to let the looks and the talk swirl about him.

As he finished eating, John became aware that they were now talking of 'plots' and 'another look along the river' and 'the potatoes need earthing up' – that was from Janet – and 'staying on watch'. Now and again one or other of them would glance towards the windows high up under the ceiling – as if, John realised, they were not trying to see out but were, rather, gauging the light. He saw with surprise that the light filtering through the growth outside the windows was fading, and guessed that he must have slept through much of the day. Janet, replying to a question from Eric, was saying: 'The moon will be coming up. We'll manage all right.'

Eric's place at the hole in the wall had been taken by the tall thin man, Duncan. The boy with near-white hair and the girl with protruding eyes were going out. Janet across the table was looking expectantly at John.

Eric asked him: 'Are you feeling youself now? I'd better explain things a bit.'

Looking at the man Eric had become, John could see little of the boy he remembered. Through the beard Eric's mouth was firmly held; there was no trace of the vague droop characteristic of the boys at the House. And the eyes under their thickened brows were more than quick and bright; a wariness lurked in them, contrasting with the relaxed looks of the others. Yet Eric's manner was friendly as he spoke of John 'needing time to get used to our ways' and requiring a trainer so as to learn what was expected of him. 'For the time being you'll work with Janet,' Eric went on. 'She'll tell you what to do, and we shall expect you to do it. If she tells you to hide, you must hide at once without question. If she tells you to separate, you must leave her. You'll be on your own then.' Noticing John's frown, Eric added: 'Janet will tell you to separate only if danger's near. It's better that only one of you is caught.'

For a long moment Eric looked at him, and John saw an indefinable glint in the dark eyes. 'You realise what you've done, don't you?' Eric asked him. 'You've run away. Of course, if you wish you can go back to your House, and if you can find the way –'

'I – I couldn't!'

'What do you mean?' Eric's tone had a slight edge to it. 'Do you mean that you couldn't find your way or that you don't want to go back?'

'I – I couldn't go back, not even if I could find the way,' and in his own ears John's voice had taken on an unfamiliar urgency. He seemed, too, to be speaking not from thought but from an impulse that he had not felt before... at least, not before the time when he and Janet had been hiding in the field and she had asked him if he wished he hadn't run away. Again there came into his mind a tangle of impressions: his fear as Matron's hand reached for his arm, himself running faster than he had known he could, the relief that he had incredibly survived the river's danger, the strangeness of his appreciating the cunning with which Janet had evaded the patrolling duty-men, the friendliness with which the seven of them joked and chatted... John could not put into words such a variety of new feelings. But he knew, without thinking, that he could not let them go, could not return to the dull heaviness that had filled his consciousness through the slow-dragging days and weeks and months at the House.

Eric was regarding him. 'There's much more to it than you know,' he said. 'It'll take you weeks before you begin to understand... and during that time you'll be on trial, of course.'

'On trial?' John repeated the unfamiliar phrase.

A hardness creeping into his voice, Eric asked: 'What do you think would happen if you were caught?'

Again there came into John's mind an awareness of how little he knew of the life that surrounded him. The stories had hinted of punishment for those who disobeyed; but the nature of that punishment was beyond John's imagining. Again he recalled how each New Year the oldest group of boys had left the House, had filed up the road and out of his knowledge. But they had not disobeyed. Mystery wrapped their destination but not punishment. He had run away, he and Eric and Janet and the others...

He saw the tight set of Eric's mouth within the beard. 'You would be taken to a Party-man, perhaps to the District Leader; and he would try and make you tell where you had been. He would want to know who you had been with, where you had hidden, who we are. The Party would want to catch us all and others, to take us to whatever fate they have in store for us.'

That last phrase was beyond John's understanding, but he could hear the threat in Eric's voice. He felt a chill of fear creeping over him. Just for a moment he recalled the security of the House and the life he had known. There he had never had to try to understand, to search for meanings in words and phrases, to feel afraid. . .

But even as he felt the hold of his former way of living, John forced himself free of it. The strange, sudden, new wakefulness that he had discovered in himself pulled more strongly. He knew that he had to stay.

Deep under the heavy brows, Eric's eyes were watching his face. He said, again speaking slowly: 'The Party-men may try and make you tell them, John. They may hurt you, starve you, threaten to kill you. We don't know for sure, but we do know that they would like very much to know where we live and how.' The suggestion of a smile softened his expression. 'You'll have realised that we're what you've been taught to call Lost Ones, but we're not as you expected us to be, are we? We're doing something much more than merely running away and hiding. You'll come to understand in time; but, meanwhile, you'll be on trial.' Catching John's recognition of the unfamiliar phrase, Eric added: 'That means that we'll be getting to know you and making sure that you're suitable to become one of us. When we've all come to know you better, we'll have a vote on it.'

'A vote?' John recalled Janet using the word.

'That's how we decide what to do. We haven't any duty-men or Party Leader telling us what to do, so we decide among ourselves. But until we've decided about you, you'll have to do as we ask you, and to do it without questioning. For the time being Janet will be your trainer. You remember? What she tells you to do, you must do.'

John caught Janet's smile, but now it seemed less sure.

'Do you feel like beginning tonight?' Eric asked him. And Janet added, brightly: 'It'll be earthing up the early potatoes. Sorry we haven't more exciting work to begin with!'

'All right?' Eric asked. 'Go along then – and be careful!'

So, with an abruptness that amazed him, John began his new life. In a few minutes Janet was leading the way out of the door, pausing as Ewan had done a few steps up to peer through the bushy screen at the night-wrapped trees about the place before nodding for him to follow. Again John saw a hint of uncertainty in her look. Yesterday, as they had lain in hiding, she had spoken with delight at the prospect of being his trainer; now she appeared less eager.

She whispered: 'You're in with us now, but you can still go back to your House if you'd rather.'

John stared his puzzlement.

Her voice so low that her whisper only just reached him, Janet added: 'You realise why we're working together, don't you? We're the youngest; it won't matter so much if we're caught.'

* * * * *

For more than a week the weather stayed fine with moonlit nights. At first John spent much of his days sleeping. Sometimes he awoke to find pale-haired Hugh's pink face, sullen even in sleep, on the mattress next to his, sometimes it would be red-bearded Ewan's or Duncan's long face. The three girls, he came to notice, slept in a roughly curtained recess off the main room.

After a meal at dusk, Janet led him by hidden paths to one of the 'plots'. Always, John came to realise, a plot was close to the remains of a building, a patch of cleared ground framed by bushes so thick as to make a screen. On the plots crops were growing much as on the fields about his House: potatoes already sprouting well, rows of broad beans, carrots and turnips nearly grown enough to need thinning, cabbages and lettuces to plant out; and inside a nearby ruin was a hiding-place for the tools, many of them old and, John guessed, collected from the decayed buildings round-about.

Having for so long worked under the eyes of duty-men, John could not at once adapt to his new circumstances. He began working slowly, ploddingly, as he had always done; and then, abruptly, he would become aware of Janet's warning stare as his hoe jarred on a stone and so broke the night's stillness or she would look sharply at his slowness. Not for three or four nights was he able to begin to match her cautious deftness. He became aware, too, that always she was listening to the sounds of the night. At first, he turned quickly to her at any whisper of noise. . . until he came to interpret the creak of a tree, and the ruffling of the dead leaves as a fox or badger or cat passed on its hunting through the bushy growth, and the soft swishing of branches stirred by the night breeze. He came also to gauge the distance away of a patrolling van. Though both of them stopped work at the sound and stood listening, John soon realised that the patrols went regularly, usually along the roadway that followed the valley, twice each night up one of the two lanes that climbed through the waste of trees and ruined buildings to gain the hilltop.

For the most part he and Janet worked silently. Only when a sound had startled him did Janet whisper reassurance, only when they finished work as the night faded, and hid away the tools, did she comment shortly on what they had done. But as the succession of working nights lengthened, questions began forming in John's mind. He became increasingly aware of the fragments of buildings about each plot; they seemed to spread over the whole hillside. He had seen similar ruins standing among bush-clumps or half-hidden by trees when, at the House, he had walked with the other boys to a Celebration; but then he had accepted such sights. Now he was coming to see that the buildings must once have been complete, and that people must have lived and worked in them. Yet all now stood empty and looked to have done so for many years. . . and he found himself recalling old Duty-man Ben telling of 'a long time ago' when 'much happened that's best forgotten' which seemed to link with the numbers nineteen ninety-seven. Sometimes, as he and Janet paused briefly in the work, he looked at her, thinking to voice his questions; but her eyes were often intent upon the shadows among the growth fringing the plot, forbidding talk.

Once his growing curiosity demanded expression. They had stopped work to eat a potato-and-bean cake and then had scooped up a little water from a stream which trickled alongside the plot. As the water's earthy coolness recalled the first such drink he had taken, John looked around and again saw the jagged walls rising up into the moonlight. He had to whisper: 'Those buildings: people used them once, didn't they?'

Janet looked sharply at him. 'There are so many of them,' he added, 'all empty.'

'You'll come to understand,' she replied, her look uneasy. 'You can't expect to know everything all at once.'

Returning each morning through the fading darkness to what John was coming to think of as 'Base', they found a meal waiting. John scarcely noticed that nearly always the food was potato and broad beans, until one daybreak Hugh returned with two rabbits he had trapped. All were delighted at the prospect of a change; and when, next morning, John met the unusual flavour, Eric smiled at his expression. 'They still don't give you much meat at the House?' he asked. 'It must go to the Party and the duty-men.'

Yet, though he had contributed to the rare change of diet, Hugh appeared dissatisfied. 'We could have pig if I could go over towards Chesham,' he told Eric.

Eric looked at him sharply. 'We've had that out before,' he said.

'But they're wild!' Hugh protested. 'They must have got away –'

'So you said about the chickens,' said Eric as if to end the conversation.

But Hugh went on, his pale eyes sullen: 'Well, they were

in the wood! How was I to know they'd strayed from a House?'

The others were looking at Hugh, at the anger glowing in his eyes and deepening the colour of his face; and John, noticing, recalled that on the day of his escape Janet had spoken of Hugh as if she disliked him. John could not remember her exact words. . .

'Look, Hugh! You know what we've decided!' Bitterness rather than anger sharpened Eric's voice. 'If we can't live without taking from others' work as the Party does, what are we trying to do? I know potatoes and beans get tedious, but with the summer coming we'll soon be getting the new crops. Why not go along the river and try for wild duck, or over by Hemel for rabbits? You're a hunter, and a good one – or you'd never have been able to live on your own for so long. But you agreed before we accepted you that you'd give up stealing – yes, stealing! – hens that you knew had strayed from a House, and pigs, too. It's no good now pretending that you thought they were wild. We cannot allow that kind of thing, that pretence!'

Into the sudden silence, Duncan, standing at the hole in the wall, added in his gentle voice: 'It's on pretence that the Party has been built. They pretend that what they're doing – keeping everybody quiet and working – is what's good for all of us.'

John looked from one to another of them. He saw the flush on Helen's round face, and Ewan's unusual scowl, and Gwen's eyes seeming to reach towards Duncan with a look he could not interpret.

'Let's have no more of it, Hugh,' said Eric, his tone easing a little. 'You know the consequences. . . and we're all grateful for the rabbit.' He turned to Ewan: 'Take a turn on watch, will you? Duncan must be hungry.'

*   *   *   *   *

During that time of working by night, sleeping by day, John did not see much of the others. Often one or two of them would be still out when he and Janet returned to

Base; sometimes he awoke to find only two or three in the main room, and one was always occupied in staring into the hole in the wall. Had John dared, he would have asked about that strange pastime; but he had come to feel that any expression of his rapidly growing curiosity might be unwelcome. Though their friendliness persisted – Ewan was always ready to help him, Helen often smiled as if in encouragement, and even Gwen's stare appeared less critical – yet sometimes they would break off their light, easy-sounding talk, or turn it to another matter, as if they were being careful of what they said in his hearing. Again and again he recalled Eric's phrase 'on trial'; he was becoming increasingly aware of what it implied. Not until several weeks had passed could he be truly accepted.

And during those working nights he was gathering a host of impressions, was seeing things he had never before noticed: a badger going nose-down and purposeful on its nightly foray, the pale shape of an owl flying in utter silence just overhead, the jerky bounding of a hunting weasel. At first he felt only the excitement of discovery, and turned quick-eyed to Janet whose smile in reply was often amused at his interest. But soon John was coming to realise that such sights were only the more memorable moments in the spring life and growth everywhere about him. Sometimes, as he straightened his back while planting more potatoes or thinning a turnip-row, he would look about not only at the ruins and the shadows but at the bushes and trees reaching up into the moonlight. And he saw, as if with newly-opened eyes, the multitude of growth, every branch and twig sprouting with new life. . . until he came to appreciate that about the plots thrived a host of living things of a variety and wonder that in his dulled life at the House had never penetrated his consciousness.

John's new-found awarenesses seemed to become almost tangible when, one afternoon towards dusk, Duncan suggested that he took a turn 'on watch'. Already, having heard the phrase many times, John had associated it with the dark hole in the wall at which Duncan so often gazed.

John had come to realise that Duncan was in some way apart from the others, separated by more than his gentle thoughtfulness. The others looked to him for special knowledge. When some question arose – to John it seemed usually concerned with 'what the Party might be up to' or the water-supply or about 'ideas they had in nineteen ninety-seven' – all looked to Duncan for help or explanation, and Duncan's eyes would narrow as if in concentration . . . though when he spoke, what he said usually had little meaning for John. He caught unfamiliar words like 'telephone' and 'electricity' and 'machines'; Duncan seemed to associate them with the Party or with how people 'had lived in the past', and again John would become aware of the many questions that had been gathering below the surface of his mind, and wonder when he would begin to gain some understanding of the strange environment in which he had come to live.

When, that afternoon, Duncan had called him over to the hole in the wall, John went quickly, hoping that Duncan might be about to explain. But, instead, Duncan nodded towards the hole and said: 'Take a look in there.'

John looked into the dark hole – and gasped in astonishment. He seemed to be looking through the wall but seeing not the earth that he knew must be on the far side of it but over the remains of nearby buildings and over treetops to a distant length of roadway that somehow appeared startlingly clear. He almost jumped back from the hole, fearing that the wall had lost its solidity; and then turned amazed to Duncan's smiling eyes.

'You'll soon get the way of it,' Duncan said. 'It's what was called a periscope. I found out about it in an old book. It goes up the chimney.'

'But how – I mean, I saw outside and – and so far –'

Duncan's smile deepened. 'That's the idea. You can see what's happening outside without being seen. Keep looking. Now, put your hand on this knob, and turn it slowly. . .'

John gasped again as the scene through the wall slid to one side, and a field rose up, a field with animals looking like sheep; but a mistiness was intruding.

'Turn that other knob if it's gone out of focus,' Duncan told him.

The view became clear again, but it had changed. Beyond the sheep a file of figures was walking, little figures like boys and a man beside them. John blurted his amazement: 'There's some boys and a duty-man! It's as if they're near!'

'They're going back to their House,' said Duncan easily. 'It's just over the hill.'

'But how can you see. . .?'

'I'll explain one day,' said Duncan. 'You keep watching. Try moving a knob now and again –'

'There's a van, a big one!'

'Let me see.' Duncan took his place at once. 'It's only a supply van. . . You know what a patrol looks like, don't you?'

'Oh yes. It's much smaller, and dark grey.'

Duncan nodded, and again John looked into the viewhole. He turned the knobs cautiously, seeing the scene change, become misty and then clear again. He nearly exclaimed as he saw another van going along the roadway; but he realised in time that it was not a patrol. Then he saw a third van and after a space a fourth. There were more vans than he had realised, and in more sizes than he had noticed before. Then, suddenly, a pigeon landed on the branch of a tree nearer at hand – John almost cried out at its abrupt appearance – and he saw that the topmost branches of the tree were sprouting new leaves. He turned a knob and found his way back to the roadway. It was clear but the shadows across it were blurred. John twisted the other knob until he realised that the low sun had gone behind a cloud. . .

Some time later he heard Janet's voice and turned briefly to smile his huge excitement. He was aware that others had gathered. He heard Hugh saying grudgingly that it was about time John made himself useful and Ewan's easier tone adding that he had done well. But John was too concentrated on the view-hole to catch more than a few random phrases of their conversation: 'a scatter hide. . . he must have somewhere. . . Do you remember Edward's hide? You used to go there. . . we haven't got anywhere else at present. . .'

Staring into the view-hole, John was beholding a bewildering series of happenings. He had lost count of the number of vans of varying sizes that had passed along the road, though he was sure he had not missed seeing a patrol. And often his attention had been caught by other sights among the trees about Base. He had seen blackbirds fluttering as they sought roosting places, and an owl pale against a tree-trunk before it flew off to hunt, and a blue-tit searching late for insects on a twig, and – remembering to watch the roadway – he had seen a fox trotting along it, unconcerned that a van had just passed. And all about, as the last of the sunlight seeped through gathering clouds, he had caught again and again the new growth, each tree, each branch, each twig thrusting up its contributions to the spring life. But now, curiously, the sights seemed to be awakening a response from deep within him, to be making him feel that, in some indefinable way, he was part of the immensely varied living panorama. He felt, suddenly, a surge of hope that this strange, exciting way of living could go on and on –

A movement on the roadway snatched his thoughts back to the moment. 'There's a patrol!' he blurted.

Duncan was at once beside him. 'Let me see.'

John watched as Duncan bent to the view-hole. For a moment John felt alarmed; he had been so intent on all that was to be seen and felt that he might have overlooked the dangers –

'It's all right,' Duncan smiled. 'It's the regular patrol, and it's keeping to the main road. . . You've got the idea quickly,' he added, 'but you've had long enough. Hugh, would you take over for a while?'

With a feeling of disappointment, John relinquished his place at the view-hole. Then he saw that Helen was holding out a plate of potato-and-bean cakes to him. 'You've not eaten anything,' she said, and her smile was encouraging. 'As soon as it's dark enough, Janet has to show you your scatter hide.'

Seeing his puzzled look, Janet added: 'It's where you'll have to go if we have a scatter. If a patrol comes too near and looks as if they might go searching. . . You'll have to watch where we go so that you'll know the way.'

Again John felt himself understand more quickly than would have seemed possible only a few days ago. He realised that on a scatter he would be on his own. 'How long will I have to stay there?' he asked Janet.

'I'll explain when we get there.'

After the sun had sunk behind thickening cloud, Janet led the way. As John followed through thickets, past the darkening shells of buildings, across what had been a roadway up from the valley, he kept watching for guiding sights – the lean of a tree-trunk, the shape of a staring window-space, a recognisable cluster of bushes – that would, he hoped, remind him of the route. After some minutes Janet stopped at a low building which, as a large portion of still intact roof showed, had never had more than one storey.

Janet climbed in and walked across the broken floor. Under a hole in the ceiling, she looked up. 'Good, the rope's still there,' she whispered.

Through the gloom John saw her reach up and pull at something too slight to be a rope. At once a rope fell dangling through the hole. John realised it must have been guided down by a string tied to a nail on the wall.

'Can you climb it?' Janet asked him.

She went up quickly, hand over hand; as she was reaching the ceiling John noticed how her feet gripped the rope. 'Come on up!' she whispered through the hole.

John grabbed the rope and tried to pull himself up. Somehow he caught the rope between his feet, forced himself upwards until she was pulling at his arm. He managed to struggle through the hole.

'You'll have to come again and practise,' Janet said. 'Now, up with the rope.'

Lying on the ceiling beams under a fragment of roof, she pulled up the rope. John saw that she coiled it neatly, leaving the string still through the hole, ready for the next time it was needed. Again he felt admiration of the way she – or, more probably, Eric or Duncan – had anticipated future needs.

Janet seemed in no hurry to return. 'We'll wait till it's dark,' she whispered. 'If we have to scatter, you run here. Do you think you could find the way?'

John was not sure. At first they had followed the route to one of the plots, but after that. . . he recalled a crooked tree, and a broken length of wall. . .

'You'll have to try again in a day or two,' Janet said.

John ventured: 'How long would I have to stay here?'

'I'll show you.' She squirmed round on the beams that held the ceiling until she could see through a break where the tiles had fallen from the roof. 'See that chimney near the dark cypress tree? Near the top, there's the signal.'

'A signal?' John had never heard the word.

'The things you still have to learn!' John caught her smile. 'We've all had to, so don't worry!. . . Can you see a bit of wood sticking out near the top of the chimney?'

John peered through the fading light. 'I think – oh, yes!'

'That's the signal. Duncan fixed it up; he's clever at such things. . . When it's sticking out, it's all right. But if anything's wrong, Duncan will make the signal drop. That means don't try to get back to Base until it's dark, and then go carefully.' Janet laughed softly. 'That's the idea, anyway. The other week the wind blew the signal down, and Helen and Ewan had to stay in their hides all day – at least that's what Helen said when they got back. That reminds me.'

She felt between the ceiling beams and found two bottles.

'The water will be stale by now. This hide hasn't been used since Edward.'

'Edward?' asked John. He could not recall having heard of him.

'They caught him. At least, he didn't come back. It was my first scatter; I didn't understand much.'

John was realising that not since the day of his escape had Janet talked so freely to him. On the plots there had been the risk of being overheard, at Base she had seemed, like the others, to hold back from speaking much with him. But now relaxed, her small face wearing its easy expression, John felt he could risk asking a few of the many questions that had come to him. 'You mean that Eric – or anyone else – doesn't know what happened to Edward? He would have been. . .' John tried to reckon. 'Well, Eric's and Ewan's year. If they'd caught him, they wouldn't have sent him back to a Boys' House.'

Again he was groping among the fragmentary memories from his life in the House, recalling that every now and again – after each New Year's Celebration, he thought – the boys whose names began with the earliest letter had been marched away; and then, later in the day, new young boys had arrived. Each time John and the others had been allotted fresh bunks and had changed their places at the Meal table. He had assumed that the young boys had come, as he himself could dimly remember doing, from a Mothers' House; but where the older boys had gone. . .?

'What would have happened?' he asked suddenly. 'I mean when I was old –'

Janet's sharp stare stopped him. 'Did you have to shout like that?' she whispered fiercely.

John had to go on, though he lowered his voice: 'I – I've never thought about it before. The boys who left each year: where did they go? Does Eric – or Duncan – know what happens to them?'

'They go to work for the Party.' Janet's whisper had a hardness to it. 'They have to make what the Party needs:

clothes and machines, and vans and tools and – and such things. Lots of people have to do it, every day, with duty-men or women watching them. It must be worse than working in the fields! Duncan says there's a place over at Hemel where they work, and another near Chesham, and more in London.' And then, her brightness suddenly returning, she added: 'Why worry about that? We've got away from it all!'

Her quick change of mood suggested that at any moment she would be evading the flow of questions her words had prompted. John asked quickly: 'Would we all have to go to such a place if we were caught? Would you – and Helen and Gwen? I mean, there are Mothers' Houses.'

'They're not for us! Eric reckons only the duty-women and the Party ones are allowed to breed. He says that part of the trouble in nineteen ninety-seven was that there were too many people.'

John frowned sharply as he tried to grasp what might underlie her lightly spoken words; but before he could phrase his feelings into words, she added quickly: 'It's time we were getting back. It's quite dark.' Already she was climbing through the hole in the ceiling. 'You'll have to hang on and drop. Mind the floor!'

John had to follow, squirming to the hole, lowering himself through it.

'All right?' Janet whispered as he landed on the broken floor.

'Yes. I – what you were saying just now –'

Her quick look checked him as if she feared he was about to ask more than he could yet be told. But suddenly she was whispering: 'Why worry about that now? We've only got to keep out of the way of the Party for a year or two, and then we'll be able to go beyond the Marsh. That is, if I decide to ask you –'

'Beyond the Marsh?' John held on to the phrase. It suggested that somewhere, in some remote place beyond the Party's reach, Janet saw the new, hopeful, exciting way of living going on.

'You'd better forget I've told you about that until we've voted on you,' Janet said; and then, more easily: 'Why worry now? We've alive! Isn't that enough for the time being?'

John caught the eagerness in her voice. It strengthened the feelings that had grown so speedily in him. Following her as she slipped from shadow to shadow, he felt that in some as yet incomprehensible way Janet was part of his awakening to the life about him and the hopefulness it brought.

5

Glimpses of the Way Ahead

THE weather changed. One morning as John and Janet returned from a plot, they saw the sun rising with sparkling brilliance, but within an hour it had been blotted out by clouds, and John fell asleep to the sound of rain pattering heavily on the weeds outside the high-up windows. When, in late afternoon, he awoke it was still raining and through the next several days heavy showers were frequent.

At first John was surprised that the others seemed delighted. At the House a rainy spell had meant additional, protracted Lesson Times where the only change from the slow chanting of the familiar stories was an hour-long session of laboriously copying some pages of them. But at Base the rain was welcomed after the dry weather. There was talk of 'having a bath at last' and Gwen particularly was 'tired of her hair feeling such a mess'. But for the first few wet days Ewan smilingly warned that there was as yet not enough water.

John had learnt that Ewan was in charge of the water-supply collected in old barrels set where a sufficient portion of roof drained into them, and supplemented by a pipe which had been contrived to lead down to Base from a pond a little up the hill. Now and again, before setting out for a plot, John had been asked by Helen to fill a bucket, and he had taken to getting some for himself to wash in – and had been warned by Ewan to go carefully with it. But so much had been new to him during those days that John had thought little beyond the immediate tasks, though now he realised that he would like to have a shower such as he had had twice a week at his House.

However, Ewan declared reluctantly that they would have to wait until the water-barrels were fuller. 'Meanwhile,' he added, 'first things first. There's the loo-site to change.' His smiling eyes turned to John. 'Would you give me a hand? You'll have to learn about such necessary jobs.'

John followed him out into the grey raining day-break, each taking a spade from the stack of tools just inside the door. Outside, along the fragment of wall, Ewan looked around and selected a spot where a thick, sprawling bush offered shelter. 'As I dig,' he said in a low voice, 'you shovel the earth into the old hole. With luck no patrol will come looking so early on such a day.'

John nodded. As with Janet, he set to work steadily, unspeaking.

By full daylight Ewan had dug a sizeable hole and the old one was all but filled. As they paused for a short rest, John had to lift his face to the rain, to feel it trickling down his cheeks, to catch it with his tongue. It was the awakening water that he had first drunk at the spring beyond the potato-field fence.

He heard Ewan chuckle. 'Are you thirsty as that?'

'Not really. It's what it means, somehow.'

'I know,' said Ewan. 'We've all felt it – often. It's being alive and feeling you've something to hope for.' He leaned on his spade-handle in the shelter of a bush already thick with leaves. 'I remember the first time I felt it,' he went on, smiling a little wryly. 'I was standing at the top of a field, and it was raining, too. I had to roll down the field – yes, roll down all the way through the wet grass! I got soaked and I nearly got caught, too. Luckily David pushed me into the ditch before the patrol came round the corner.'

John risked asking: 'David?'

'He's gone on,' said Ewan.

John wanted to ask him what he meant, if the David he spoke of had 'gone on' to where Janet had referred to as 'beyond the Marsh'. But he recalled the way Janet had often turned the conversation as if to avoid his questions, and he looked away from Ewan. Seeing again the ruins rising above the tangle of growth about Base, John ventured a less direct question: 'All those buildings: people lived in them once, didn't they?'

Ewan seemed not to mind his asking. 'Yes, a long time ago.'

John caught the echo of Duty-man Ben's words when he had asked the old man if he had lived in the House when a boy. He recalled, too, the numbers the Party Leader had used at Celebrations as if implying a time in the past, a time measured in years. He asked Ewan: 'Was that in what's called nineteen ninety-seven?'

Ewan looked at him, an appreciative warmth in his eyes. 'You're coming to understand quickly!. . . Yes, it was all of thirty years ago. There was a lot of trouble; I don't know much about it except what Old Potter has told us. The people then – they must have gone mad. They fought among themselves. They had things called bombs; they'd destroy buildings and – and roads. Some people escaped, but many. . . It was then that the Party got control. I suppose they had to, at first; but that was years ago, thirty years at least.'

He stopped speaking, and John caught his unusual frown. 'We'd better get the hut into place,' Ewan added, 'and stick grass over the old hole in case a patrol starts looking.'

Like Janet, Ewan seemed to have turned the talk just as more questions – Who was Old Potter? What had driven the people mad? Where had they gone? – had come into John's mind. Yet Ewan's manner, more relaxed than Janet's, suggested not so much reluctance to talk but, rather, as if he could only guess at possible answers himself.

* * * * *

While the heavy showers persisted work on the plots became reduced to infrequent early hours of planting out and weeding until, within a week, the ground was too sodden to work. The eight of them had by then taken to sleeping more at night, remaining awake much of each day and spending their time on necessary tasks in or around Base. Only towards grey, dripping dusk was it reckoned safe to venture far. Twice John led Janet to his scatter hide to make sure he remembered the way and to refill the water bottles; but each time Janet seemed reluctant to stay there long. Though her phrase, 'beyond the Marsh', with the stirring suggestion of ultimate escape from the Party kept recurring to him, John felt he could not risk making her uneasy by directly questioning her. Indeed, her frequent unwillingness to say more than was immediately necessary made him feel more strongly the significance of Eric's phrase 'on trial'.

Late on another afternoon of misty rain he and Janet went to the river in search of ducks' eggs. On the way they came on a patrol van unexpectedly; it was halted half-hidden by a hedge and, had they not heard the men's voices while still at a distance, they might have approached dangerously near. As it was, Janet was for once taken by surprise. 'We'd better separate,' she whispered. 'Go along that hedge – and keep down! I'll be along the river. A willow juts out. . .' And she slipped away.

As he made his cautious way behind the hedge, John felt tension rising in him. It was the first time he had not Janet's guidance, and the hedge was low and broken in places. Once he had to dart across a gap through which the patrol could have seen him. He dropped behind a thin remnant of hedge and lay still, listening. He felt his heart thumping as he peered around through the grey light for a way to run at the first sound from the van; but there was no movement and at last he crawled on to where a hollow, thick with weeds, led down towards the river. As he crept more stealthily than he could have thought to move only a week or two earlier, he heard the van start up, and at once held himself still, listening intently above the renewed pounding of his heart. But the van was moving away and, as the last sounds from it dwindled, a feeling of triumph stole through him. He had, on his own, defeated the patrol!

Reaching the river, he saw the tree leaning over the pale water; but Janet was not there. Aware of a building – a House it looked like – standing above the field rising from the far bank, John moved cautiously along beside the river, keeping to what cover the rushy growth provided. He heard, some distance ahead, a flurry of movement and the sharp quack of duck, and recalled the purpose of their expedition. As he went on he kept watching – and so came on a swans' nest. But the birds, stretching their great wings and hissing threateningly, showed that he could not plunder them without much disturbance. Then, beyond a tangle of bushes at the water's edge, he saw Janet. She was wiping herself with her tunic. 'Didn't you think to have a bath?' she asked as he reached her. 'You have to take a chance when you can. Ewan says we won't have enough water for days yet.'

Scowling a little, John wondered if he should risk the river; but it was nearly dark and the story's warning still lingered. As he turned away he noticed a drake, its neck broken, lying at Janet's feet. Catching his stare, she said casually: 'It's quite easy when you know how, and you have to get meat when you can. . . The eggs are hatched,' she added, 'so the duck will look after the little ones.'

John felt his sense of achievement at dodging the patrol dwindling. In his new way of living he still had much to learn.

* * * * *

During those days while they waited for Ewan to declare that there was sufficient water for a bath, John came to realise that others also had special tasks. Though all joined in such daily work as preparing food, Helen was in charge of the stores, including the wood gathered in hiding-places roundabout – more than once John had to search for fallen branches that could without much risk of drawing attention be broken and added to the bush-screened piles. Gwen saw to the clothing, patching when necessary or making replacements out of pieces of fabric that were still to be found about the ruined buildings. She was also responsible for the sandals, the soles made from plaited rushes sewn into a foot-like shape, the straps from rabbit skin or other material that had been found. Duncan, when he was not peering into the view-hole, was often at a recess filled with all kinds of strange objects: coils of wire, lengths of piping in several sizes, two instruments like those John had seen duty-men talking into, boxes with a conglomeration of coloured wires fixed in them and one with a glass front, many oddly shaped and pierced pieces of metal, and all so randomly stored that once John heard Gwen protest to Duncan that he would never be able to find what he wanted. 'You've not tidied it up since David went on,' she said.

John guessed from the confused collection that it must be Duncan's special job to devise such things as the signal and the pipe from the pond and the still incomprehensible view-hole. John overheard him talking to Ewan about 'finding out how to pass on messages', and was reminded of the morning of his escape when the duty-men had been so mysteriously able to summon Matron. Catching John's curious glances, Duncan had smiled and asked him to 'keep his eyes open for any metal things. We've been looking for years,' Duncan added, 'but you never know what's still to be found. They had a lot of machines and gadgets in the old days, and we know that the Party have managed to keep some of them working.' Often, John came to notice, Duncan would leave his recess and, taking one of several tattered books, would squat near a high-up window, apparently reading the small words or puzzling over the strange, lined drawings. Had he dared, John would have asked Duncan what he was trying to discover; but though Duncan's quiet manner did not suggest that he would be rebuffed, John restrained his curiosity.

At last, after a week of heavy showers which at times became an hour of steady rain, Ewan announced one daybreak that a bath was possible. Calling to John and Hugh to help with two buckets each, he led the way to the first of a succession of water-barrels. Following Hugh back with a full bucket in each hand, John found that against the remaining above-ground wall of the building stood a small room, its window blocked, all but hidden by a cluster of sycamores. Inside stood a low container as long as John was tall, into which Hugh was emptying his two buckets. As John went to tip his, Hugh said sharply: 'You weren't expecting a nice warm shower like at your House, were you?'

'I hadn't thought –'

'You'll get used to it. . . And you'll have to wait until last!'

It took many bucketfuls before the bath was judged full enough. Ewan produced a kind of yellowish clay. 'It's the best we can do for soap,' he told John, 'until Duncan can make something better. It gets the worst off.'

Despite Hugh's assertion Ewan, as if allowing the others to enjoy his handiwork before himself, waited until last. John waited with him while one by one the others, each provided by Gwen with a fragment of old tunic or blanket, disappeared to return a few minutes later, their hair clinging wetly, rubbing themselves dry. As Janet reappeared, Ewan nodded to John. 'Enjoy yourself,' he smiled, 'but not for too long.'

Inside the little room John found that the bathwater was already yellowed from the 'soap'. Getting into the sudden chill, he recalled Hugh's words about 'a nice warm shower'; but as he rolled himself about, the water's coldness seemed to start a warmth inside him. It was, again, the awakening water. He tried a handful of the clay, rubbing it on his skin and into his hair; then, reaching his head back, he washed it out. All the time he felt the water about him, cold and enlivening, unlike the soft warmth of the showers at the House. Never before had he been able – or even wanted – to immerse himself, to feel the water's penetrating freshness. . .

'Are you going to be much longer?' came Ewan's voice;

and John looked up into the man's amused eyes. He guessed that Ewan was remembering the first time he had felt the awakening water swirling about him.

After the meal, John helped Gwen with sandal-making. He had looked hopefully towards the view-hole, but Duncan had asked Janet to take a turn for, it seemed, the pond-linking pipe was giving trouble and he and Ewan soon left to clear it. Eric was already out; John had come to notice that he might disappear for a half-day or a night, and had linked his goings with overheard phrases such as 'keeping in touch' or 'seeing what's happening'. Hugh was also out, visiting his traps; that seemed to be his special activity.

Sitting across the table from Gwen and Helen, John kept his eyes on his work, for he had learnt how critical Gwen could be and, though he had gained a fair skill at plaiting the rushes, fashioning the long strip into a foot-like shape he found tricky; and once he had broken a needle and had speedily learnt from Gwen's sharp annoyance how precious were the few that had been found. Helen was drawing strands from a piece of old cloth for use as sewing thread; but, that morning, she was more concerned about her other duties. It seemed that they were running short of fat. 'I'll be able to manage the cooking,' she said to Gwen. 'But the lamps won't last much longer. Whoever goes next to Old Potter will have to ask if he can get some.'

John recalled Ewan mentioning Old Potter. He kept his eyes on the sandal-sole.

Gwen said: 'Perhaps whoever goes next may find a stray sheep or a pig. You remember that when Ewan and I last went, we saw a sheep along the Old Way – in the woods so it must have been a stray.'

'I remember.' Helen smiled as she wound her thread. 'And you didn't manage to catch it though there were two of you!'

'It would have been a weight to carry all the way back.' Gwen's tone was casual. 'We told Old Potter, of course.

Perhaps one of the groups around there had more luck and they've got fat to spare.' As Helen glanced at her, Gwen added: 'It'll be more your worry than mine. Eric will surely have agreed by next winter! I was old enough to go on a year ago!'

'Hasn't he said anything yet?' asked Helen. John heard a hint of uneasiness in her voice.

'He'd rather I asked Ewan,' Gwen replied reluctantly. 'Of course he can't say so, not straight out. And as you know, Ewan might not be willing.'

John wondered what she meant; she sounded as if she expected Ewan not to want to go 'beyond the Marsh'.

Helen began: 'Eric must want Duncan to stay on here for as long as possible. There's so much he understands –'

'He'd be even more useful there,' Gwen interrupted. 'He was saying the other day that he's heard they've got power working. Duncan would be able to help with that.'

As he reached for another length of thread, John noticed that Helen looked as if she found Gwen's words disturbing. He had an impression that his presence prevented her from saying what was in her mind.

Gwen, as if following her own thoughts, went on to Helen: 'I wonder what it'll be like, living in a family group, I mean. Do you think about it much, or haven't you got that far?'

'Of course I think about it,' Helen said. 'It's not so long before I'll be old enough.'

'I suppose much of it will be like here,' Gwen said; 'growing our own food and making our own things and so on. And we'll have animals and hens as well. But we'll be expected to have babies, too.'

Helen looked quickly at her. 'Surely you'd like that!'

'I suppose so, when the time comes. If it was sure to be Duncan going with me –'

Gwen suddenly realised that John was sitting across the table. 'Haven't you finished that sole?' she asked him; and then, her voice even sharper: 'I don't know! You take long enough to learn, and then –'

'Don't be too hard on him,' Helen interrupted, flushing. 'It's only a few weeks!'

John bent over his work, aware that Gwen's eyes were still on him as he struggled to sew the plaited straw into shape. But he found it difficult to concentrate, for he was wondering if Gwen's annoyance had been prompted not by his slowness but, rather, to cover her own carelessness in letting him overhear what he should not yet know. She and Helen must have been – could only have been – referring to 'beyond the Marsh'. Again he found himself recalling the idea that had come to him when Janet had let slip the phrase, the possibility that they would be free of the Party. . .

His thoughts were diverted by Janet at the view-hole saying: 'There's a patrol. There are two vans.'

'Two of them?' Gwen looked sharply at her.

'They've stopped,' Janet added, still peering. 'They've stopped near the bottom of the lane.'

'I'll tell Duncan,' said Gwen, and made for the door.

John had come to know that patrolling vans usually went singly. He looked at Helen, but she had turned to Janet. 'Keep watching,' she told her. 'They'll take a minute or two. . .' She began to gather up the work. 'You put your things in here,' she added to John, opening the door to a low cupboard, and he realised she was preparing to leave as little trace as possible that they were living there.

Janet said: 'They're talking to one another. They're looking up this way.'

'Will we have to scatter?' John asked Helen.

Helen said calmly: 'We may.' And then: 'You go. If it isn't a scatter, it'll be practice for you.'

After a quick glance towards Janet still staring into the view-hole, John went. As he peered through the growth before climbing the steps, he saw Ewan returning and assumed that Gwen and Duncan had already gone to their scatter hides. He slipped quickly and quietly through the rain.

John reached his hide without alarm. He was just at the window-entry to the low building when he heard a van begin to grind up the lane that passed near his hide. He scrambled in and, pulling the string, brought down the rope. He had climbed up under the roof, was coiling the rope, before the van was near.

Then, abruptly, the van stopped. John lay tense, head down; but after several seconds, as the van did not start again, he risked looking around for a way of escape through the roof. If the duty-men should think to search –

With a crunch the van restarted. As John listened to its grinding persistence, he became aware that he was trembling. Almost outside his hide the van's sound changed and he feared it was about to stop again; but it went on, and John heard, like an echo, another van making its way up the lane on the far side of the Base.

As at last the sounds moved away, he could relax and more than relief stole over him. He had been on his first scatter, and had evaded danger. It had really been far easier than he had expected. A thrill of achievement mingled with cunning. Not for a moment could the heavy-moving, slow-thinking duty-men have guessed that they had passed within a few paces of him. And to think that only two or three weeks ago he would have blundered about and so betrayed his presence! He had now, he knew, little to fear from such dull men.

As he lay awhile, relishing his newly acquired skills, the conversation he had overheard between Helen and Gwen came back to him. He felt again the hopefulness that his growing awareness of the spring's growth had brought, but now it was greatly strengthened. To think of being able to go on living in his new freedom. . .!

Yet he was aware that Gwen had implied more. She had spoken of 'family groups', hinting of a way of living very different from both the life he had known at his House and the way the eight of them were now living. And, adding more puzzlement, Gwen had sounded as if she was not thinking to 'go on' alone; she had spoken as if she wanted to go with Duncan, and as if Eric preferred that she went with Ewan. John recalled, too, the uneasy look on Helen's face. Had that been prompted by Gwen saying that Duncan would be helpful to the people 'beyond the Marsh', or by Eric's wish that Gwen should go there with Ewan?

Other recollections were mingling with his thoughts: Janet, when she had spoken of 'beyond the Marsh' saying something about 'if she decided to ask him' and, still further back, on the day of his escape, speaking of 'not having to go with Hugh'. At the time the phrase had been meaningless; but now he realised that Janet, like Gwen, had been implying that when the time came for her to 'go on', she would not go alone. Perhaps, as around Base, they had each to help the other to avoid dangers?

The idea stirred his imagination. He saw himself and Janet dodging patrolling duty-men, making their way across unfamiliar land reaching towards a huge spread of rushy growth like an immensely enlarged version of the fringes of the only river he knew. He saw them coming at last to a great, dark, spreading waterway sufficient to stop the patrol-vans. . .

His vision abruptly blurred as he thought of their having to face such an obstacle. How would they evade its dangers, how would they know where to cross it?

Suddenly he recalled 'Old Potter'. Gwen had gone on from speaking about him to talk of 'beyond the Marsh'. The two must be linked! Old Potter must know the way to get there, the safe route through. He must be the means by which they could make their final escape from the Party, the means by which all of them could go on enjoying this exhilarating way of living!

Hopefulness surging up in him, John suddenly wanted to be back at Base; and, recalling the signal, he squirmed round to look at it. To his surprise it was up, as if there had not been a scatter at all, as if the others had remained at Base. After listening to make sure that, beyond the birds' songs and the pattering of the rain, there were no sounds of danger, he climbed down from his hide and made his way back.

The others looked amused that he alone had gone on a scatter. 'You've had a private one of your own, eh?' chuckled Ewan.

Through his warm hopefulness John recalled the thrill of hiding while the duty-men passed. 'They stopped almost outside,' he said. 'I thought they were coming in.'

Ewan's smile faded. 'Did you see why they stopped?'

'I – I didn't try to look.' Surely, John thought, Ewan did not expect him to risk moving while a patrol was near.

When, a little later, Eric reappeared, he seemed to share Ewan's concern. He also asked John if he had seen why the van had stopped.

'It could have had difficulty getting up the hill,' Duncan suggested.

Eric appeared unable to accept such an explanation. 'There were two vans,' he reminded Duncan. 'They must have been working together. It looks as if they're changing their routine.'

To John Eric looked more than concerned. The line of his mouth held a hardness, almost a bitterness, and the dark eyes glinted. It was as if Eric was stirred by more than the need to keep free of the patrols and the Party until the time when he could 'go on'. The others – easy, friendly Ewan, tall, gentle-voiced Duncan, kindly Helen, quick Janet, even Gwen despite her frequently sharp looks, and Hugh despite his habitual sullenness – had escaped to enjoy their freedom; no doubt they, like John now, were deep-down excited by the prospect of their way of living continuing and developing 'beyond the Marsh'. But Eric seemed to be moved by other feelings. Could it be that he intended to stay at Base, helping others on the way of escape while he continued to pit himself against the Party? As the idea came to him, John felt that such a role suited Eric more than the strange life about which Helen and Gwen had spoken.

6

The Voting

SEVERAL times within the next few days two patrolling vans appeared together and drove up the lanes climbing the hillside, one keeping to the lane beyond Base, the other grinding up past John's hide. It was as if the patrols were watching the area of tangled growth and ruins from either side. Each time there was a scatter. As the others left Base, John went quickly to his hide, climbed into the roof, and lay listening to the vans' progress; but not again did he hear a van stop and, after perhaps an hour, the signal showed that it was safe for him to return.

With the others, John felt growing uneasiness to which the persisting rain, keeping them much inside Base, added a sense of restriction. Clearly the patrols were changing their pattern of working and that disturbed Eric. He went about Base, his eyes hard, his mouth tight, saying little to anyone but Duncan. 'If it was later in the year,' John heard him say, 'we could leave here. There must be safer places further out; but with the crops not yet grown. . . '

Duncan appeared less anxious. His long face wearing its usual thoughtful look, he suggested that perhaps the time had come to consult Old Potter. 'He'd know somewhere that another group has given up,' he said. 'If it was near enough for us to come back and gather the crops. . .'

Eric seemed uncertain. 'He might suggest that we split up; and as it may all be a false alarm. . . A patrol may have seen someone, one of us perhaps. They may just be taking a look.'

His uneasiness spread through the others. To John, Ewan seemed at times preoccupied, Janet spoke little, even

Helen's smile became less ready. Gwen appeared ever more restless; once John overheard her say to Helen that she 'didn't want to be caught after all this time. In another month or two I'll have gone on.' Only Hugh seemed little moved, though John heard him say to Duncan that he could 'give them the slip by moving over towards Chesham'.

Then, one grey, dripping morning, Ewan at the view-hole saw only a single patrolling van, and it took the former route along the valley. Later that morning another patrol appeared alone, and again during the afternoon. It began to look as if the former pattern had been resumed; and when, during the following days, no more than single patrols were sighted, the feeling of tension eased. Sharing the relief, John realised how tightly the uncertainty had gripped him; for over a week he had felt scarcely able to think on his hopes of 'beyond the Marsh'. So often had his attention been diverted by trying to interpret through the steady rain every unexpected sound, every hint that the patrols might be seeking them, that any thoughts beyond the immediate present seemed unreal.

When at last the danger seemed past, the rain too had eased. It became again possible to work on the plots. A new moon was swelling, giving enough light to make fresh sowings of carrot and turnip, and the planting of French beans and more potatoes; and Ewan and Gwen were to join in the delayed work. As John set out with Janet, he felt his hopefulness reviving. The past ten days had emphasised the dangers through which they would have to live before they were old enough to 'go on'; but they had survived them and, as John reflected as he began to thin a row of lettuces, Ewan and Duncan, and Helen and Gwen, had contrived to keep free of the Party through at least two years. Surely he had already proved himself as capable of dodging slow-moving, slow-thinking duty-men!

Adding to the feeling of relaxation during the next days, their food became more varied. Thinnings from the earlier turnip and carrot rows gave a welcome additional flavour to the potato-and-bean cakes, and two nights in succession Hugh returned from his traps with a rabbit, and once brought a pheasant. Each time it seemed to John that the others were excessively delighted with Hugh's achievements as if they were trying to lift the sullenness that often shadowed his pale eyes. Yet Hugh did not look pleased with himself, and a little later John heard him say to Janet that 'it was easy over towards Chesham. . . We could find somewhere there,' he added. 'We could manage all right.' John saw Janet stare sharply at the boy, and again recalled her earlier reluctance at 'going with Hugh'.

Then, on a dull, drizzling afternoon, there came another alarm.

John had slept late and had awoken to find only Hugh sleeping in the little room. As he went towards the main room, he had heard Gwen's and Duncan's voices, but they stopped as he went in. As usual Duncan was at the view-hole, but Gwen, at the table mending a tunic, looked up sharply as if annoyed with John for interrupting them. He had the impression that they had been arguing, and almost at once Duncan asked him to take over the watch, and went out.

As John peered through the grey light at the traffic along the valley road, he recalled again Gwen's hope that she would 'go on' with Duncan; but soon thought of her became submerged by renewed amazement that Duncan could have contrived so helpful a device as the view-hole. It seemed almost a let-down that this afternoon there was no patrol to watch, only the usual bulky store-carrying vans with an occasional smaller one, no doubt on Party business. John did not notice that Gwen had gone into the curtained recess that the girls used as their sleeping quarters until he heard her exclaim: 'He says Eric wants him to stay on here a year longer! Eric seems to think he'd find some way to make electricity and save us having to rub sticks every time we want a light! Duncan's clever, but that's a bit much to expect!'

John heard Helen reply: 'I should think the Party would be on to us if we got electricity.' She must, John guessed, have been facing the curtain for her voice to have reached him.

For a few moments neither of them spoke; and then Helen went on: 'You said the other day that Duncan believes they've got electricity beyond the Marsh: do you think they can have done?'

'Why not?' Gwen's voice was still sharp.

'Well, if they had, wouldn't the Party stop them using it?'

'How could they?' asked Gwen. 'They couldn't drive their vans through the Marsh!'

Though he tried to keep his attention on what was to be seen through the view-hole, John frowned in puzzlement as Helen went on: 'How can you – or any of us – be sure about that? I remember reading a story about a girl rescuing a duty-woman who'd lost her way and had been caught in a swamp. That's what the story called it, but the picture showed a lot of water and mud and rushes. And a van came to help them. It must have been able to get there.'

'That's only a story!' Gwen sounded almost contemptuous. 'You know they were to make us believe that the Party was all-powerful! The way they used to say that we'd starve if we ran away!. . . And besides, the river that goes through the Marsh – what's it called –?'

'The Seventh River, isn't it?'

'It swamped all the land roundabout years ago, and brought down the bridges that were still left, Duncan says. That would stop the Party going there – if they ever wanted to!'

John was so intent on what Gwen and Helen were saying that he felt a sudden alarm when he saw through the view-hole that a patrol van had stopped on the valley road near where the lane led up towards Base. As he stared, he caught Helen saying something uncertainly about 'the Party going there'.

'That was years and years ago!' Gwen replied tersely. 'That was before the Seventh River flooded! I know that we used to think that the Party could –'

John saw a second van stopping behind the first. 'There are two vans!' he called.

At once Helen and Gwen came out. 'Two of them?' Gwen asked, and John, too, felt a return of his fears of ten days ago.

Then he saw a third van drawing up behind the others. 'There's another! They've stopped at the bottom. They look as if they're talking to each other!'

'I'll tell Duncan and the others!' said Gwen. 'You do the signal!' And she ran out of the door.

As Helen went and moved a strip of wood fixed to the chimney, John saw that Janet had appeared. 'What do I do?' he asked her. 'Do I leave the view-hole?'

'You'll have to,' said Janet. As she turned to the door, Helen said to her: 'Ewan's up at the pond. Your hide's that way if he doesn't notice the signal –'

John looked at Helen as Janet went out. 'It's a scatter all right,' she said. John followed Janet out and turned towards his own hide.

He was barely halfway to the low building when he heard a van start up the lane. He felt himself tighten at the sound; but, as he went on, he heard the van stop. His momentary alarm was checked; he continued on his way quickly, knowing that he had only to reach his hide to be safe from the duty-men.

He had climbed into the building, had pulled down the rope, before he heard the van start up again. Steadying another tremor of alarm, he climbed into the roof. Yet before he had coiled the rope, the van again stopped. And then he heard another van, climbing the lane on the far side of Base, also stop, while the third sounded to be moving a little further off before it, too, stopped.

Lying in his hide, John felt his heart thumping as he heard the nearest van restart and then, after perhaps a half-minute's grinding, stop again. He realised sharply that the duty-men must be stopping every few paces to look around the nearby ruins. As yet they were still well below his hide; but if they came nearer, if they should look into the building. . .

With an effort he kept hold on his rising fear. The confidence he had acquired during the past weeks helped him to think, to begin to shape his danger. First he noticed the rope lying in its coils and realised that a duty-man might see the guiding string. He reached his hand through the hole and with a tug broke the string; if a duty-man should think of looking under the roof, John would have some seconds' warning. Then, as the van ground to another halt – and it was unquestionably nearer – John looked out through the gaps in the roof. One showed an area of sparse weeds and stony ground offering no chance of quick cover. Another gap overlooked an ivy-tangled bush reaching almost to the eaves. If he had to escape he could drop into that bush's thickness –

A movement in the thicket beyond the bush snatched his attention. A white-haired figure was moving not twenty paces from his hide. John's mind jumped to the District Party Leader with his thick, white hair above the penetrating eyes; yet he knew that the head he had glimpsed had moved too furtively, and it was making not for the van but, rather, as if to avoid the duty-men. Then, just as the van started again, John remembered Hugh. In the grey, rain-smeared light his pale hair would have looked as white.

The van rumbled nearer through a long half-minute before again crunching to a halt so loudly that John knew it must be almost outside. He lay trying to still his trembling legs as, above the noise of a more distant van climbing the hill beyond Base, he heard sounds of thrusting through the bushes about the building, then the unmistakable scrape of footsteps at the decayed doorway, then a grunt as the man must have stumbled on the rotted floor inside.

'What a mess! Look out, or you'll fall through the floor!'

John's hold on his shaking body was almost broken by sudden alarm at the sharpness of the man's voice. He had spoken as quickly as Ewan or Eric. He was no slow-voiced duty-man.

'Any sign of them where you are?' the man asked, it seemed to John from only a pace or two from below the ceiling hole. Another quick voice, less distinct as if the speaker was still outside the building, replied: 'No, though it looks as if someone's been here. This can't be the place though they might. . .' The second voice became muffled as if the man was moving away.

The man below John said suddenly: 'There's a hole in the ceiling. They could have climbed up.'

With a great effort John held himself from jumping up and scrambling through the gap which offered a way of escape. He caught the second voice again, but it was too indistinct for him to make out the words. The voice below him went on: 'It looks as if someone's been in here recently. It might be worth bugging, so that if they come again –'

The other voice interrupted; but again John could not catch what the man said. He seemed, however, to have annoyed the one standing in the room below. 'I know the orders!' he replied sharply. 'Though why the Party doesn't let us round them all up and be done with them. . .' The man was leaving as he spoke; his last words were confused by his movements across the rotted floor.

A few seconds later John heard above the pounding of his heart, the van start up and then, perhaps twenty paces on, crunch to a stop. Again he heard, more distantly, another van echo the sounds. They must, he realised, be searching all the buildings. For a while he lay still, a feeling of chill stealing over him. Would the others avoid capture as he had done? What if they, like himself, had been assuming that they had no more formidable opponents than slow duty-men, and had relaxed? What if Janet or Ewan or Eric were caught, if when he returned to Base he found the place empty?

Not for some minutes during which he became aware that the vans were haltingly moving away, did John recall what he had overheard. . . and he began to realise that he had been so intent upon his danger that he had not concentrated on the exact words. An impression persisted that the men, whoever they were, had been not so much looking for him as searching for Base. One had said something about 'this not being the place', and the other had spoken of doing something – the phrase escaped John – 'in case they came again'. But stronger in his recollection was the sound of their voices. He recalled Janet's saying, on that first day at the spring, that duty-men were 'too slow'. He realised that the duty-men he had known had probably been 'kept quiet' as the boys in his House had been. But the men he had overheard – could they be those called 'Party-men'? – had sounded as alert as he had become.

Even after the last sound from the vans had been lost in the noises from outside – the rain now swishing through the leaves, the flutter of a bird alighting on the roof, a thrush's leisurely song – John moved only to make sure that the signal was still down. Remembering the bottles he and Janet had refilled, he reached for one, telling himself that the water would keep away his hunger as well as his thirst; but the now-familiar earthiness, recalling by contrast the sickly-tasting water he had known for so long, brought an awareness of how near he had been to discovery and, probably, a return to the dull restraint which had for so long been his experience of living.

At last the hostile sounds had faded beyond the reach of his hearing. After a while, he looked again towards the signal and saw that it was still at danger. Though the sight told him nothing certain, he felt easier; at least none of the others had too readily left their hides. Relaxing, he found himself visualising the others still, like him, waiting in hiding. Janet's hide would be small, a little corner where she could curl up in safety. Ewan's would be a larger place to suit the impression of stocky strength, while Duncan's would be high, befitting his tall, thin body. Helen's hide – John smiled to himself at being able to play such a game after his recent alarm – would be larger than Janet's with space for her to store food in neat piles. And Gwen's. . .

Though the impression of Gwen came at once into his mind he could not imagine a hide for her. The sharp restlessness so often in her protruding eyes made her appear as if she was always looking beyond the present, beyond the confines of Base or, now, of her hide whatever it was like. It was as if she was always thinking of the time when she would be 'going on'.

The thought brought back the conversation he had overheard between her and Helen, and uneasiness began to steal his feeling of relaxation. Helen, usually appearing composed, had unexpectedly spoken as if she feared that they might not be safe from the Party 'beyond the Marsh'; she had even said that the Party had been there. Gwen had, John remembered, tersely dismissed such an idea – 'That's only a story!. . . The Seventh River swamped all the land roundabout years ago, and brought down the bridges. That would stop the Party!' – yet recollection of the tone in which she had spoken now suggested that Gwen could have been not so much downing Helen's uncertainties as trying to hide her own.

Scowling, John tried to push away the thought. Surely, he told himself, Helen must have been mistaken, must have still been influenced by the memory of an old story that had been deliberately intended to make them, as children, accept the Party's powers. He recalled briefly how fearful he had been of the river on the day of his escape. Surely, if there was any reason to believe that the Party's power could reach beyond the Marsh, Eric and Duncan would have known. And Old Potter, too; whoever he was and whatever part he played, it would all become purposeless if the Party could –

A movement from below, not a rat scurrying, snatched John's thoughts back to the present. He held himself still,

his hearing reaching down into the darkening room below.
'John?' came Janet's whisper.

At once he was letting himself through the hole. As he landed beside her, Janet said: 'Duncan's signal hasn't worked again!' Though she spoke lightly, John thought she looked uneasy as she led the way back to Base.

The lights in their saucers of fat had not been lit. Following Janet in, John saw through the darkness the faces turned towards them. He glimpsed near-alarm in Gwen's eyes, and an unusual tautness on Duncan's face. Then he realised that Ewan and Hugh were not there.

Eric asked him in a hard voice: 'Hugh was asleep when you had to scatter: did you think to wake him?'

'No. I – I didn't remember –'

Helen said: 'I told John to go.'

Through the darkness John saw Eric turn to her. 'I'm not blaming – anyone!'

John suddenly remembered. 'I saw him. . . at least I think it was Hugh. His hair was nearly white. I thought at first –'

'Where was this?' John felt rather than saw the sharp look in Eric's eyes.

'Soon after I got to my hide. I heard the van coming. It sounded as if they were searching so I looked out to see where I could get away. And then I saw him, just for a moment – at least, his hair was nearly white.'

Eric's look seemed to be piercing into John. 'But weren't you using Edward's hide?'

'Yes. At least you said the first time –'

Janet's voice, tighter than John had heard before, interrupted: 'Yes, John has Edward's old hide.'

'But that's the other way!' began Gwen.

Eric asked John: 'Are you sure it was Hugh?'

'I – I thought at first it was the District Party Leader, the one who used to come to our House. His hair looked white. But the van was coming up the lane on the other side, and he moved as if he was keeping out of sight, and he wasn't so tall. . .'

From the view-hole Duncan's voice came with gentle irony: 'I can't imagine a Party Leader trudging about on such a day!'

John wanted to tell what he had overheard while in his hide, but at that moment Ewan came in. 'He's not there,' he told Eric. 'As far as I could see, he hasn't been in his hide at all. The water bottles are still full.'

For a long moment no one spoke. John felt their concern, but to him it seemed excessive. Hugh could have found the way to his hide blocked by a van and so have been compelled to take refuge elsewhere. And surely it mattered little beside what he had overheard. He ventured: 'I heard two men. They came into the building –'

Eric turned at once to him. 'Did you hear what they said?'

'Yes. And they weren't duty-men, not like at the House. They spoke much quicker and –'

'They certainly weren't duty-men,' Eric interrupted. 'The Party is serious this time. What did they say?'

'I – I can't remember exactly but. . .' John was aware that all their eyes had turned to him. 'It was as if – as if they were not looking for me, but trying to find out where we lived.'

Eric flashed a look at Ewan. 'Did they say anything else?' he asked John.

'One of them said something about the building – where I was – not being the place though he had seen someone had been there. And he saw the hole in the ceiling. I thought he was going to climb –'

'What else did he say?'

Over Eric's shoulder John saw that Duncan had turned from the view-hole to listen, and across the table Ewan's eyes were intent on him. 'I can't remember it all,' John struggled, 'and one of them – he didn't come so near. The first one said that we might come there. Then the other one said something I couldn't hear. It seemed to annoy the first one; he said something about knowing the orders, but he sounded annoyed because the Party wouldn't let them catch us. . . or something like that.'

'You're sure of that?' Eric's tone was sharp. 'You're sure he said about the Party not wanting them to catch us?'

'I'm not sure of the exact words, but that's what he meant.' As he spoke, John frowned at the strangeness of it; surely, if the Party knew they were among the buildings, they would have been intent on catching them?

Eric had turned to Ewan. 'It's as I was saying: they want to watch us for a while, and then. . .'

Gwen asked suddenly: 'Are you sure. . . about the man you saw coming out of here?'

'Of course I'm sure!' Eric's tone was hard. 'I don't have to be near enough to see his badge before I can recognise a Party-man!' As John stared in sharp astonishment, Eric added to Gwen: 'We may as well have some light. There's no point in sitting in this gloom.'

'But they may see –' Gwen's alarm matched John's.

'Does that matter now?' A note almost of resignation had crept into Eric's voice. 'They know we're here. If they'd wanted to catch us, they could have waited until we came back one by one. . . Helen, have you got some food ready cooked?'

As Gwen lit a light, John caught Helen's wide-eyed amazement. 'You mean we're going to stay?'

'We'll have to risk it. If what John overheard is any guide, they don't intend to catch us for a day or two.'

Gwen began: 'But why –?'

'They're probably hoping we'll all take fright and dash off and so lead them to other groups.' After a moment, his look hardening, Eric added: 'And it'll give us time to deal with Hugh.'

As Helen set about getting the meal, Duncan asked Janet to take over the view-hole. Then he came over to John.

'How long were they in your hide?' he asked him. 'Could they have fixed up some wires or anything like that?'

'I don't think so. They weren't there for a minute. . . as if they knew it wasn't the place they were looking for.'

'Did they say anything about needing a telephone or electricity or power?'

John shook his head. 'No. I'm sure I'd have remembered.'

'What can they be doing?' asked Gwen, her eyes seeming to protrude the more with her anxiety.

Eric said: 'Before we eat, all have a good look around. I know we've looked already but now we've got some light. . . Ewan, will you search the bathroom? You, Gwen, have another look in your recess, and John make sure there's nothing in your room. There's just a chance that they may have fixed up some wires or a trap or – or something.'

John went and looked about the little room he shared with Ewan and Hugh. The mattresses on the floor and the stools appeared untouched; and there was nowhere anything could have been hidden. Yet John felt uneasy; the Party might possess powers he could not even imagine.

He returned to see Duncan and Eric standing by the recess in which Duncan kept his collection of strange objects. They were looking at a small, round metal box that Duncan was turning over in his hand. 'I don't remember seeing it before,' Duncan was saying, 'but as you can see there are all kinds of bits and pieces in there.' He nodded towards his recess. 'Most of them were there before I came, you'll remember. David must have collected them, and Edward used to find quite a lot.'

'Where was it?' Eric asked him.

'Down by that box thing. It could have been there for years.'

'But surely you'd have seen it!' exclaimed Gwen.

Duncan smiled at her. 'You yourself were saying, only the other day, that I never clean up the place.'

Gwen did not respond to his easy manner. 'It can't be one of those things the duty-women used to talk into, can it?'

'A telephone, you mean?' Duncan said. 'There's one over there: it's got a bit to talk into and a bit to listen. It's nothing like this thing. This hasn't any way to fix wires, and telephones had to have wires to carry the electric power.'

Gwen persisted: 'What about those other things they had: radio, wasn't it called? Could it be. . .?'

Duncan shook his head. 'They had to have electric power, too. They had to be plugged into power in the houses or have what they called "batteries". And, anyway, they were much bigger than this.' He turned the little box over. 'I'll try taking it to pieces tomorrow when I can see what I'm doing.'

Eric had turned towards the table. 'Let's eat,' he said. 'We've got other things to sort out, more urgent things.'

As soon as they had sat down, he went on: 'This is what I suggest: First, we can't risk leaving Hugh on his own; he may go back to his stealing habits, and if the Party should catch him. . . You and I, Ewan, will look for him first thing tomorrow.

'Next: you, Helen, will have to get enough food ready to last a day or two. You'll help her, Gwen? Then I suggest that all of you go to your hides and lay up there until dark tomorrow. And we'll all keep our eyes and ears open – we must find out what they're up to! Then, if it's still safe, we'll all meet here. From what John heard, they don't intend to catch us – at least not at once. But they may change their minds, and come marching in here as soon as it's light. If you see any sign of that, or anything else that looks unsafe. . . well, there's only one thing to do: make your ways singly to Old Potter and tell him what's happened.' He looked from one face to another. 'All agreed?'

Ewan said 'yes', the others nodded. But uppermost in John's mind was bewilderment about what he might have to do. He had to ask: 'Old Potter? I – I don't know where he lives, and if I can't come back here. . .?'

Unexpectedly Eric smiled. 'We're forgetting you. Yes, that puts you in an awkward spot if the worst happens. Can we assume that all this upset hasn't put you off, hasn't made you change your mind about becoming one of us?'

'Oh no!' Though he was sharing their uneasiness, John answered at once.

'Do you know what you're letting yourself in for?' Eric asked.

'I know a little. I – I've heard about going beyond the Marsh and – and that there are people living there like us but differently. And I know I mustn't tell the duty-men – or the Party-men – anything, whatever happens. And there are other groups like us, but I don't know where they live or – or how to find Old Potter though I think he must know the way to get –'

'You've kept your ears open,' interrupted Eric. He looked at Duncan and then at Ewan. 'What do you think? It's too soon I know, but we can't leave John with nowhere to go if the worst happens.'

Gwen asked sharply: 'Do you mean to vote? But it's only a few weeks! Always before we've waited much longer: two or three months. And there's Hugh; he may come back and – '

'We can all guess how Hugh would vote,' said Eric, a bitter note again in his voice.

Ewan said: 'It's hardly fair to John otherwise.'

'Is it fair to John to insist?' asked Duncan. 'He can't know much of what he's letting himself in for.' He turned to John, his thin face troubled. 'You'd have to live like this, dodging the Party-men, somehow getting your own food. . . It's not so bad in the summer, but when winter comes. . .'

'And you'd have to wait two or three years,' added Eric, 'and all that time you can never be sure what will happen. Much of the time you'll be afraid that the Party will catch you, trap you, somehow get you back.' His dark eyes were fixed on John's face as if watching for any sign of wavering.

'And there's the Island!' added Helen, a flush on her cheeks and her look anxious. 'I'm not thinking that John wouldn't do – he's done very well so far. But he ought to know that if he should do anything we can't accept. . .'

John remembered Janet mentioning the Island, a place where he could be left to look after himself. Eric went on: 'You realise, John, that if we find we cannot trust you, if you let us down, we would have to take you to the Island. There you'd be on your own. You'd have to find what food you could – and when the duck fly away and the water freezes there wouldn't be much to find! If you could get away – and the path through the Marsh is hard to follow – the only hope for you would be to get to a House. Even if you could find another group they'd never trust you once they knew you'd let us down.'

John wanted to reassure them, but Eric's words about the Island checked him. When Janet had spoken of the place, it had meant little to him; now, having come to know how much he depended on the others and the way of living they had fashioned, he felt the utter loneliness and the dangers of being condemned to live at the Island.

But as he began: 'I – I must stay with you! I wouldn't –' Gwen broke out: 'It's not only that! He's too young to understand all that the Party –'

'He's Janet's year,' Ewan interrupted. 'We trusted her; we can trust John.'

'How do we know that?' Gwen demanded. 'How do we know if the Party caught him. . .? I'm not saying that he would mean to tell them anything, but how can we be sure?'

'You can't be sure of any of us,' said Ewan. 'We all think we wouldn't say anything, but until we're tested, until the Party does whatever it can to make us talk, how do any of us know what we would or would not say? None of us can be sure, even of ourselves.'

Duncan nodded. 'We have to trust each other. The thing for John is whether he can trust us.' He turned again to John. 'You do understand about the Island? We'd have to take you there if you let us down; and more than likely if you tried to get away you'd get lost in the Marsh.'

'I think I understand,' John said. 'And I wouldn't let you down, I'd never tell the Party-men – anything!. . . And I couldn't go back, not now.' John caught sight of Helen's face, concern overlaying her usual smiling friendliness. 'I – I wouldn't do anything,' he added, 'not to let the

Party or – or anyone – find out about anything!'

'We know you wouldn't mean to,' said Helen, trying to smile. 'But there's so much you can't understand yet. And to think of the Island –'

Eric said abruptly: 'Let's vote on it.' He turned to John. 'That'll mean that we've decided to trust you – or not as the vote goes. It'll mean, too, as Duncan has warned you, that if you let us down. . .'

Gwen still looked alarmed. 'But if he knows the way to Old Potter, and the Party catches him –'

'It's not fair to leave John with nowhere to go if we have to leave here,' Eric replied firmly. 'Old Potter can surely look after himself – he's been doing it long enough! And we must tell him what's happened, and you know what we've agreed about the youngest.' Gwen looked as if about to protest again, but Eric added: 'Get out the sticks, then!'

Still looking troubled, Helen opened a drawer in the table. Eric said to John: 'You'll have to look the other way. . . or, better, take over the watch from Janet.'

As he went to the view-hole, John saw Helen take out from the drawer a small box containing a handful of sticks, some short, some longer. Janet at the view-hole smiled, her eyes bright as they had been when she had hoped Eric might make her his trainer. Then as he looked into the view-hole, John was aware that the six of them were seating themselves around the table. They sounded to be doing something with the sticks. As John's eyes became accustomed to the night's rainy thickness, he heard Eric ask: 'Got two each?. . . Right, pass the box round.'

They seemed to pass the box from one to another. Every now and again John heard a faint rattling as if each was dropping a stick into it. Then Eric said: 'All voted?. . . Now, we'll see.' The rattling was repeated more distinctly as if Eric was emptying the box on to the table. 'Four to two in favour,' Eric said. 'Well, John, you're one of us!'

John snatched a look over his shoulder. On the table lay

six sticks, four short, two long. He recalled what had been said about voting, and understood. Just for an instant he wondered whose the second long stick might have been but, as he caught Ewan's twinkling eyes and Janet's smile, he let the question go.

Eric came over to him. 'Keep watching,' he said, 'but listen. As soon as Helen's got the food ready, you'll go to your hide and stay there until tomorrow evening. Keep watching while you're there – we must try and find out what they're up to. . . Tomorrow evening, or perhaps the evening after – I'll let you know – you and Janet will have to go to Old Potter and tell him what's happened. You'll have to try and remember the way – Janet'll help with that. It'll take you a night to get there and another to get back.'

Eric paused a moment and though John kept his eyes on the view-hole he knew that Eric was looking at him.

'As you've probably realised,' Eric went on, 'Old Potter is a kind of link between the groups of us – and with the people who have gone beyond the Marsh. He has to know what's going on; he may be able to tell us where we can set up another Base – if we have to. And he has to meet the people we may be sending him in a few years' time for him to pass on. And, of course, if we have to leave here suddenly. . .'

Eric's voice was easier, but John heard the warning in it. He felt that out in the dark, raining world beyond the shadows he could see through the view-hole, the Party's threat was growing.

'We'll all be trusting the two of you to get there and back,' Eric added.

'Yes. I – I mean, I'll try all I can.' John wanted to assure Eric again that if he should be caught he would tell nothing to the Party. But with a nod Eric turned back to the others.

John glanced momentarily from the view-hole. He saw that Janet was helping Helen with the food. She gave him a look, quick as ever but a little uncertain. It might have been only the uneasiness that all were sharing; but as he stared again into the view-hole, John recalled her saying when, on the first night of his strangely new life, they had set out for a plot: 'You realise why we're working together, don't you? We're the youngest so it won't matter so much if we're caught.' And Eric, a few minutes ago, had reminded Gwen of what had been 'agreed about the youngest'. John could guess what the uncertainty in Janet's look meant.

7

The Trial

A full two hours to dawn, John again walked quickly and silently to his hide. He noticed that the rain had eased, but the dripping darkness brought little relief to the feelings which had come to him at Base. That the Party knew of the place, that a Party-man had been inside even though he may have done nothing there, had stolen any sense of security; and it made the darkness, until an hour or two ago protective, seem threatening. Even now there could be watchers within it, and not slow duty-men but Party-men as alert and as cunning as John had become. Indeed, once John thought he heard a sound from a ruin some fifty paces from his route. Instinctively he stopped, rigid, intent; but the place was too distant for the sound to have been definable through the rain dripping from the leaves. At last, even more cautiously, he went on.

Reaching the low building, John felt relieved. His hide had already proved its safety and he could hope that, unlike Base, the building was of little further interest to the Party-men. But halfway across the broken floor he suddenly recalled how, just before the Party-men had come in, he had broken the string which brought down the rope. He could not get up to the hole in the ceiling.

The realisation brought his fears rushing back. He tried to tell himself that he could easily find another hiding-place, but he felt how much he was on his own against dangers he could not foresee. During the past weeks he had relied much on Janet and, behind her, on the others and the way of living they had collectively created. Now, because of his own thoughtlessness – though at the time his breaking the string had seemed a precaution against discovery – he could not do what was expected of him, could not hide where, if one of them needed to contact him, he could be found. That he had, so short a time ago, been voted one of the group brought a feeling almost of guilt.

He knew he was exaggerating. Only a pace away a dark doorway offered the possibility of another hiding-place from which he could listen, should any of the others come; yet he did not at once go to it. As he stood uncertain, the silence beyond the night sounds from outside seemed menacing. Again he felt how little he knew of the ways of the Party who controlled the men he had heard below his hide and the patrols and the duty-men, and through them had controlled his every action, every thought, for thirteen years. He felt that whatever he did, wherever he went, the dangers from his ignorance would go with him; he felt, too, how brittle was the freedom that Eric and Ewan and the others had achieved.

Though aware that he might be visible to watching eyes, John had to force himself to move towards the dark doorway. His legs were trembling so that once he caught his foot on the broken floor and nearly fell. It took a deliberate effort to steady himself and go on.

The doorway opened on to a passage, to one end a door all but rotted away, to the other more dark openings giving into other rooms. John stared at them, wondering which would offer the safest hiding; then he saw a door still in place and shut. He moved to it, his ears reaching for any hint of danger from outside. The door-handle still survived and with only a faint creak the door opened to reveal, not another room, but a small, black, enclosed space, so small that he did not at once link it with the store-cupboards he had known at the House.

The darkness offered protection; yet he was hardly inside than the place felt oppressive. If anyone came and opened the door, he would have no hope of escape. After only a few moments, he crept out and began again to move about the building, looking for a less restrictive hide.

There were six rooms, all of them small. The room from which the hole led into the roof was the largest and that was only five or six paces at the longest. Even in spite of his uneasiness, curiosity began to stir in his mind. The people who had lived here must have spent much of their time apart from one another in the small, separate rooms, and there could hardly have been more than five or six of them.

He had returned to the largest room, was standing at its doorway still seeking a hiding-place; yet a deeper layer of his mind was trying to imagine how the people had lived before nineteen ninety-seven. Ewan's words about their having 'gone mad' and 'fighting among themselves' and 'bombs destroying buildings' came back to him; but he thrust them aside as he tried to visualise the people for whom the place must have been built. They must have reckoned to live in smaller groups than there had been boys in his House. There might have been boys and girls – and men and women, too, like the 'family groups' beyond the Marsh that Helen and Gwen had spoken of.

The phrase stayed in John's mind even while his eyes were searching for a safe hiding-place. The building he was now in, and probably the others whose ruins stood on the hillside about Base, could all have been built for 'family groups'. He recalled Gwen talking of 'being expected to have babies' when she went on beyond the Marsh and, more distantly, Janet saying that 'only the duty-women and the Party ones were allowed to breed'. He stood, his eyes staring about the room but feeling mounting consternation that the Party's control could reach into his own being –

A sound jerked his thoughts back to the moment. Through the pattering of rain-drops from a tree outside the window-gap had come a slight scraping noise. It could have been an animal scratching on stony ground; it could have been, more distantly, someone in one of the ruined buildings catching a foot against a snag on a broken floor. Recalling Eric's warning to keep watching and listening, he waited through several seconds; but he heard no more.

He had to find somewhere less exposed than the doorway in which he was still standing. Only the corner of the room offered: the two walls would shelter him on either side and from behind, while only a pace away was the window through which he could escape.

He squatted there, his back against the angle, his feet on a surviving floor-beam. The discomfort and the inadequacy of such a hiding-place made sleep impossible, and he pulled out one of the four cakes Helen had given him. He realised that his water bottles were up under the roof and got up to peer cautiously out of the window. Outside, between the window and the ivy-wrapped bush which would be his first screen if he had to run, a puddle formed by years of rain dripping from a portion of roof showed palely; he could make do without the water bottles. As he returned to squat again in the corner, he guessed that an hour might have passed since he had left Base, and that in another hour it would be beginning to get light.

That hour felt longer than any he had known. His uneasiness seemed to bring question after question into his mind. At first he tried deliberately to imagine the others in their hides, but this time such a game could not hold his thoughts for more than moments. Almost at once he was wondering if they could be taking turns to creep back to Base to watch through the view-hole; and from that he was soon asking himself for how long they would have to spend so much of their time in separate hiding. How long could they do so? Soon the plots would be needing attention, soon they would have to be preparing the ground for the winter crops; but how could they work with the Party so aware of them, perhaps watching all their movements?

And even if, as Eric had suggested, Old Potter could tell them of somewhere else that would suit as Base, would they be able to risk returning to gather the maturing crops? Or was Eric hoping that Old Potter would somehow arrange for them all to go beyond the Marsh? Perhaps that was the true purpose of the visit to Old Potter. Perhaps he and Janet were to be told the way to 'go on', the route through the fearsome obstacle. . .

Each question seemed to lead to another. Why should they have to wait before going beyond the Marsh? Who decided when they went? Did Old Potter? Eric had said that the man needed to meet new runaways; did he also insist that they waited for two or three years? Why should he? Could he be in some way restricted by other people, those already beyond the Marsh perhaps?

And how secure from the Party would they really be beyond the Marsh? Again John recalled what he had overheard between Helen and Gwen, and again in his mind he heard Helen's unexpected doubts and Gwen's too-ready dismissal of them. Gwen had sounded almost as if, deep down, she shared those doubts for she, too, had known that the Party had been beyond the Marsh though she now assumed that later flooding prevented them from going. But the Party had powers about which John – and probably the others, too – knew little or nothing. Could Gwen, so determined to make her final escape, be deceiving herself, be clinging to her hopes even though she must know there was always the possibility that the Party were capable of going beyond the Marsh? Or was there more than John had so far learnt? He recalled Old Potter. Clearly he was in some way their guide to beyond the Marsh; could he have devised some way to freedom even beyond the Party's interference?

As he struggled with the massing questions, John was still aware of the half-ruined building about him. It seemed to merge with his thoughts. Did the ruination that had struck in nineteen ninety-seven in some way explain what might be ahead of him? He remembered Ewan telling that it had been in nineteen ninety-seven that the Party had gained control; and since then the Party had shaped the way of living for everyone except the few who had become Lost Ones. And Old Potter, he added. When he met him, would the old man be able to explain? Could the long, dangerous wait before going beyond the Marsh be somehow bound up with what had happened so long ago?. . .

It seemed as if the darkness would never fade; and yet, when he could at last see more clearly, John's uneasiness grew. . . for he suddenly realised that not once during the long night had he heard a patrol. The Party had again, disturbingly, altered their routine.

As daylight strengthened, John risked creeping out to ease his thirst with earthy water scooped from the puddle outside; but he quickly returned to the corner to squat, listening and watching. He heard the bird-songs swelling in exhilaration and variety as if to welcome a sunny day, caught hints of movement as bird or animal sought food, heard cattle lowing distantly and recalled the field he had seen through the view-hole. . . but the only sounds of human origin were of occasional traffic along the valley road.

As the sunlight reached into the room, he crouched more tightly in the corner. The morning seemed interminable, the sunshine slanting through the window scarcely moving across the broken floor. About midday he appeased his hunger with two more potato-and-bean cakes. Later, as the afternoon warmth brought on drowsiness, his head at times drooped. . . and he came to notice intermittently that the sunlight appeared to have crept more quickly. After the last of Helen's cakes, he dozed longer and awoke astonished that the sun was low over the trees up the hill and, telling of approaching dusk, he saw a hedgehog nosing about a grassy patch outside the window. Inadequate as the corner had been, it had sheltered him through the long day. That he had been unable to reach his hide seemed of less significance, though he looked around wondering if he could use a length of wood from the rotten floor to reach the rope and so be able to retie the string. After a while he ventured into the other rooms, but saw nothing he could use without risking a noise. . . though again he found himself thinking that people had once lived in those rooms, perhaps a group of men, women and children linked into a family. The possibility stirred the consternation he had felt as, during the night, he had recalled Janet's words about what she believed would have been ahead of her had she not escaped; but by daylight his fears seemed less real. He returned to squat in the corner for a long hour until at last he saw through the dusk the signal telling that it was safe for him to leave.

Nearing the tall cypress before Base he paused, feeling unsure. No sounds but those of the night, no hints that anything unusual had happened, had reached him; yet the darkness lurking under the now-familiar bushes and bramble-clusters seemed ominous. To have heard a patrol grinding its regular way up the nearby lane would have been almost reassuring. Then he caught a movement, glimpsed Helen's fair head as she slid into the shadows about the top of the steps. After a few moments John followed.

The lights were lit. As John went in, faces turned to him: Helen's and Ewan's and Janet's. . . and then he saw, in the shadows near the view-hole, Hugh's pale head and sulky eyes. John turned quickly from him to Eric standing near. Eric seemed to avoid his questioning look. 'There's only Gwen to come,' he said.

'Here I am,' came Gwen's voice from behind John, and then: 'You've found him!'

Eric said: 'Sit down all of you.' His tone was hard and firm. 'We'll get this over as quickly as possible. . . I don't need to tell you much. Ewan and I found Hugh over towards Chesham. He had made a camp there and had a fire – in daylight, too! And he had that!' Eric nodded sharply towards something lying on the floor. 'Yes, it's a young pig, and it's no wild one as you can see for yourselves. Hugh had a piece of loaf and some hens' eggs, too, but those were smashed as he tried to run from us.'

As Eric looked around the watching faces, John detected anger in his eyes and a bitter twist to his mouth. He looked away towards Janet across the table, and saw that the light, striking upwards, seemed to give an unnatural sharpness to her small face.

'There's not much else to say,' Eric went on in the same edged voice. 'Like all of us Hugh knows that the last thing we want to do is to appear as thieves, living on others' work. We'll leave that to the Party! If Hugh had had to leave his hide, to live on his own for a while, there might have been some excuse; but we know from John that he must have gone straight from here towards Chesham, that he made no attempt to go to his hide. And almost at once he began stealing to the disgrace of us all –'

'I was going right away!' Hugh's protest from the shadows behind Eric was suddenly fearful. 'I just saw the pig and – and as I'd reckoned to go on, right away –'

'Where was the pig?' Eric cut in.

'What does that matter? It was only just inside the fence if you want to know. It was coming through –'

'And the hens from whom you stole the eggs and the piece of bread?' Eric's voice was bitter. 'Were they, too, just inside the fence and just coming through?'

For a long moment Eric's angry sarcasm seemed to echo around the room. John looked quickly at the others: at Ewan with his eyes on the table; at Gwen staring into the shadows behind Duncan; at Janet, her chin lifted, her dark eyes fixed on Eric as if she was drawing firmness from him; at Helen's round face with the corners of the mouth drooping and her eyes moist.

When Eric spoke again, his voice was steady, held. 'It is as I've said before many times: more serious than the theft is the pretence. If Hugh had admitted that he had stolen, and he must deliberately have gone to a House and rummaged around for the bread and probably for the eggs . . . if he had been hungry and so had been compelled to steal, any of us would have understood though we would still have condemned it. But it is the pretence that we must think of, the way Hugh has tried to excuse what he knows to be wrong, the way he appears to expect us to accept his pretence. We cannot live here together pretending to one another. We cannot, when the time comes, go beyond the Marsh and live among the people there all the time pretending, whenever we break a rule, that we're being honest both with them and with ourselves. If we do, we shall never create there a better life; we shall repeat the conditions that brought about nineteen ninety-seven. Nor shall we be able to hope that we can overcome the Party. They at least do not pretend to themselves that they are not doping the water, not compelling people to live unnaturally. To live in pretence, to lie not only to other people but also to ourselves, would make us worse than the Party.'

No echo followed Eric's quieter tone; his words seemed, rather, to sink into the shadows. John was staring at the table, no longer able to look at the others. He felt he knew what was to happen.

'Does anyone want to say anything?' Eric's tone was almost casual. He glanced over his shoulder at Hugh. 'Do you wish to say anything?'

Hugh's pale, sullen eyes were lit with a glare. 'What's the use?' he asked; and then, suddenly: 'Don't send me to the Island! I won't go or – or I'll get away and tell the Party! I'll tell them all I know and –'

'If that's all you've got to say,' Eric cut in, 'the sooner we're finished with this, the better! Get out the voting sticks, Gwen.'

'I will!' Hugh shouted. 'I'll tell them – everything!'

'If you can get away from the Island,' said Eric drily, 'there will not be much you can tell the Party that they don't already know.'

John saw Hugh staring at the back of Eric's head; and then, as Gwen hesitated to offer the box to John, Hugh cried: 'Not him! He's only a kid and he hasn't joined –'

It was Duncan, sitting beside John, who interrupted him. 'John's one of us now. Your vote would have made no difference.' His voice sounded to John even more gentle than usual. Duncan went on to John: 'You take one stick of each size. Hold them under the table; then, when the box-lid is passed to you, put one stick in it. You put in a short one if you agree that Hugh should go, a long one if you think he should be allowed to stay. You do as you think. No one will know how you have voted, no one will blame you for the decision. Do you understand?'

John nodded. Yet, when he had taken the two sticks, when he held them out of the others' sight under the table, he wished he could tell how they were intending to vote. He looked quickly from one face to another; but all appeared strangely blank. They couldn't all be so utterly indifferent to what they might be doing – driving Hugh away, forcing him to live utterly apart. . .

Though he could not look at Hugh, John felt the pale eyes flashing from one to another of them as if unable to believe that they would condemn him, would force him perhaps to fear-filled loneliness or to return to the unknowing, unfeeling world in which the duty-men and the Party ruled. John could not bring himself to send Hugh back to that. He dropped the long stick into the box-lid and passed it to Ewan. At once Duncan was offering him the box under the table. 'Put the other stick back in it,' he said, and John heard sadness in his voice. 'It's so that none of us will ever know. . .'

The box-lid had reached Eric. 'All voted?' he asked, and tipped the sticks on to the table. There were five short sticks and two long ones.

Staring over Eric's shoulder, Hugh cried out: 'You can't mean it! It's John – he's only a kid! – and Janet, she's always hated me!'

'Will you never learn?' Eric's bitter tone cut through Hugh's wild anguish. 'It's done. If it had gone the other way you'd have accepted it, wouldn't you?' And as Hugh, his eyes dropping into a defeated scowl, drew back, Eric added to Ewan: 'Put him in the other room. We'll have to take him tomorrow.'

John felt he had to tell somebody. Hugh's fear more than his unjust accusation forced the words up in him as he turned to Duncan. 'I –'

'You don't say anything.' Duncan's voice had taken on an unusual quickness. 'You don't tell us, we don't ask.'

John turned from him to meet Janet's sharply bright eyes, and then to Eric. Unexpectedly Eric smiled. 'That's how we do things,' he said. 'When you've been with us longer you'll realise that it's the fairest way. . . It's unfortunate that your first voting should have been on such a matter, but it has to be done. By the way, did you manage to get any sleep today or last night?'

The question, suggesting that already Eric had dismissed Hugh from his thoughts, startled John. 'I – yes, I did a bit,' he stammered. 'Not in the night; in the afternoon.'

'Good,' said Eric, his tone easy as if he could not hear the sounds coming from the room to which Ewan had taken Hugh. 'As soon as you're ready – and when you, Helen, have found them half a dozen cakes each and have packed up what you can spare for Old Potter – I want you, John, and Janet to go to him. Now listen carefully, both of you. There are four things he's got to know:

'First, about the Party finding Base. Ask him if he knows what they're up to. He sometimes gets wind of how the Party are thinking. Tell him we'll stay on here a few days longer if we can. But ask him if he knows anywhere suitable for us to go.

'Second, he must know about Hugh – so that he can warn the other groups in case Hugh should try to join one of them.

'Third, tell him that, unless things go wrong, we'll be sending a pair to him later on, about September.'

John was aware that Gwen looked sharply towards Eric, but he went on:

'And fourth: we'll be needing fat for the winter, so can he contact others who have some to spare? And tell him that if the Party call off their activities, I'll try and get over to him myself. Either way, we'll get word to him as soon as we can.' Eric smiled. 'It may be you again, John, so make sure that Janet shows you the route.'

'I will,' said Janet.

'Have you both got all that?' Eric asked. 'Four things to tell him. . . and you'll have to go very carefully as you leave here. The Party must not know that you've gone. If you should think they've spotted you – well, you know how to give them the slip. All right?'

John nodded. Janet said: 'We'll get there all right; and we'll remember.' John wished he felt her confidence; so much depended on him and Janet, and she seemed not to hear Hugh's voice, duller now, coming from the adjoining room.

Eric nodded. 'You should be able to spend most of the day at Old Potter's; in fact, you'd better not start back until dusk so that you'll arrive here before it gets too light. We'll probably stay in our hides most of the time, but we'll be expecting you around dawn. . . Yes, you'd better spend the day with Old Potter so that he'll be able to tell you, John, about what happened before nineteen ninety-seven. Then you'll begin to understand.'

8

A Walk into the Past

JANET led the way. John, carrying the small sack for Old Potter, saw that she went even more cautiously than usual. Barely a hundred paces from Base she stopped abruptly, listening, making sure that no sound hinted that they might have been observed leaving. After a full minute she went on, moving quickly from shadow to shadow. Again, as they neared the top of the hill, she stopped to listen intently before taking an overgrown path along the edge of a wood.

Yet, even when they had walked in silence for most of a half-hour, she seemed not to relax. Glancing at her, John saw again the sharpness in her eyes and the raised chin; she was looking as she had done at the voting, as if she was still hearing Hugh's sudden, fearful cry as he knew he was to be sent to the Island, and his desperate, wild accusation. Until that moment John had assumed that the second long stick had been hers; now the tension on her face suggested that it might not have been. Even as the possibility came to him, his eyes were again catching through the darkness the freshness of the spring's life, and he heard a night bird hidden in a dense bush break out into rich, joyful song. The sound clashed with his recollection of Hugh's anguish.

He waited a dozen paces before he ventured: 'What do you think Hugh will do – at the Island, I mean?'

'I don't know!' Janet's voice was tight, and she quickened her step so that she was almost running. 'We don't say any more about it, once the vote's been taken. We don't think of them again.'

'Them?'

She stopped walking abruptly and looked into his face.

'Of course there have been others,' she said, and a hardness in her voice recalled Eric's. 'It's as Eric said: you can't live beyond the Marsh if you can't be trusted, if you can't help towards making a – a better way of living than the Party does, or better than before nineteen ninety-seven. It's hard to decide sometimes, but you have to!'

She turned at once and resumed her quick walk. Her tone had confirmed that she had voted to condemn Hugh. John suddenly felt that she had been deceiving him; or was it that her quick brightness had misled him. . . as Ewan's friendliness might have done, or Duncan's gentle manner, or even Helen's round-faced kindliness. All but one of them must have condemned Hugh. John began to perceive that behind their apparent ease of manner lurked a toughness, a sinewy quality of being that until this evening he had not suspected.

Janet did not speak again until, after following the path past a group of tree-shrouded ruins, they came to a lane with a clear, weedless surface telling that it was in use. Janet went to a nearby gate-post and ran her fingers down its far side. 'Feel it,' she said in a low voice. 'There's a mark.'

John felt the thin line, cut low down, pointing towards a side track. After going alongside four field-hedges the track ended at another lane clearly in use. Across it stood a group of buildings, lights showing in some windows. 'A Girls' House,' Janet whispered and, going to a tree nearby, again felt low-down in the bark. Then, with a nod to John, she climbed over a stile beginning a path that reached darkly into a wood. A short way along it they heard a van start off from the Girls' House, and stood silent until it had rumbled away along the lane they had just crossed.

After a while the moon rose, nearly full, easing the darkness. To John, Janet's sharp mood seemed to persist; he still heard a tightness in her voice as, their route beginning to descend a hill, she whispered: 'We're getting near Chesham. We'll have to go carefully. They've been clearing and rebuilding.'

A little further on she paused where a roadway led off through a tangle of trees and ruins much like that about Base. Ahead, below them, John could make out building shapes, many of them, clustered along a valley, and here and there lights pricked the darkness.

For once Janet seemed unsure. 'We'll have to risk it,' she whispered. 'There's not likely to be anyone about.'

As he followed along the side lane John soon saw what was troubling her. The lane started as if to lead through a waste of ruins; but alongside it heaps of bricks and uprooted growth showed that the land was being cleared. At one point, near a fragment of wall reaching up into the night sky, two machines stood, each larger than any van John had seen, and with great scoop-like portions attached in front of them; and beyond them four huge vans, one with its hind-container heaped with rubble and bricks, stood silently as if waiting for the men who must, only hours ago, have been working there.

As if the sights disturbed her, Janet all but ran until, two hundred paces on, they regained the shelter of more ruins. As she slackened pace, Janet whispered: 'We must tell the others. That part of the route – they're making it into crop-land. We'll have to find another way.'

On and on they went through what seemed to John an unending sequence of lane and path, through wood and along field-hedge, up over swelling hills, down into night-shrouded valleys, and always keeping away from buildings that looked to be in use. Some, John guessed, were Houses or perhaps the Party's work-places that Janet had spoken of; and, as the night passed and their way lengthened, he began to realise that such buildings, and those in ruins, spread further than he had assumed. But by then weariness and lack of sleep were slowing his thinking and blurring his anxiety. As they climbed yet another hill, he wondered if he could suggest a rest; but Janet's untiring persistence held urgency. . . until, perhaps four hours after they had left Base, she stopped where a pond showed palely through the lane-side hedge. 'We've made good time,' she said, her voice easier than it had been since they had started out.

She squatted beside the pond and pulled out a potato-and-bean cake. Sitting munching beside her, John felt his tiredness growing though it did not submerge an awareness that the place was exposed and high up. Beyond the pond a field reached only a short way before tilting out of sight. Across a dip, a wood spread darkly over a sloping hillside; behind them, across the lane, the land appeared to drop.

As if following his thoughts, Janet said: 'We're nearly at the top. Down the other side is the Old Way. We'll make it easily before it's light. You can have a sleep if you want to.' Seeing his wearied surprise, she added: 'I'll keep watch.'

John scowled. Did she never tire, he wondered. Then, having finished his cake, he scooped up a handful of the earthy water. He squatted again, staring at the pool and wondering how it came to be so high up. . .

* * * * *

A patter of chill water on his head started John awake. Through the gloom he saw Janet standing at the edge of the pond, her hair hanging wet, in one hand her tunic as if about to dry herself, the other hand reaching down for more water to awaken him. As she caught his startled look she laughed. 'It was too good to miss,' she said. 'If you want a bath, you'll have to be quick.'

John saw that behind her dawn was lightening the sky and that the moon had disappeared. Janet added: 'We must get to the Old Way before it's really light.'

He struggled to his feet. His legs had become stiff from the night's chill. As he scooped up water to banish his drowsiness, he heard distantly the sound of a van. Janet was at once dragging on her tunic and trews. 'Over there,' she whispered, nodding towards a thick part of the hedge; and as they lay behind it while the van's rumble grew louder, she added lightly: 'Lucky for me they didn't come a minute or two before. It's prickly here.'

They lay still until the van had passed and its sound was

fading. 'With luck we won't meet another patrol,' Janet said.

Within a few minutes' walk the lane led sharply downwards, twisting through what John recognised in the thin light as a beech-wood clinging to the slope. 'We'll be there in time,' Janet said.

'At Old Potter's?' John was expecting that it would take most of the morning to get there.

'Not yet. At the Old Way. . . Do you think you could find your own way, if you have to come alone next time?'

John frowned at the thought, recalling that several times Janet had checked their route by a mark cut on a gate-post or on a lane-side tree; but his weariness had jumbled his memory.

She laughed softly at his uncertainly. 'You'll remember if you have to. This is only my second time. We'll soon be there!'

The eagerness in her tone recalled the day of his escape when she had hoped Eric would accept him and that she would become his trainer.

The lane began to level as it emerged from the beeches. Ahead, as far as John could make out in the slow-growing light, an unexpectedly flat landscape stretched out into the greyness as if the hills had been abruptly cut off. Out on the plain he could see dark clusters, perhaps woods, perhaps buildings. But as the lane reached the first fields, Janet said: 'Here it is!' and turned aside into a wide, grassy track.

John guessed that it must be the Old Way, and that patrols were unlikely to use its uneven route. Between thick, straggling hedges, it appeared to follow the foot of the hills' abrupt final drop. At Janet's suggestion they ate another potato-and-bean cake as they walked. The light was strengthening behind them, and John noticed that to one side fields were to be glimpsed through an occasional thinning of the hedge, to the other the woods clinging to the hills' slope gave a feeling of protection.

The track rose gently over a swelling of the ground, the last reach of the hills. In the growing light finches darted blue-grey and gold and pink about the thick hedges which were becoming not green but white. And then the sun broke through the lingering greyness of the night, spreading its rich light along ahead. . . and John saw that the flanking hedges were of hawthorns, every branch, every twig, unbelievably vivid with white flowers.

Janet, too, was caught with the wonder. 'We had a may-tree near our House! And I've seen others, but I'd never noticed, never realised. . . It goes on and on!' The almost dazzling whiteness reached far ahead as the Old Way kept to its gentle course. 'It was still winter when I came before.' she added. 'I didn't notice, didn't expect –'

With a catch in her voice, Janet's mood changed. 'To think how blind the dope made us! When we were children we weren't allowed to see – anything like this! We couldn't see it, not really!' And then, abruptly, her delight returned and she ran a few paces, almost dancing. As she looked back at John, her dark eyes were lit with a warmth that, bewilderingly, reminded him of the duty-women when, after a Celebration, they stayed on at the Local Centre.

'We mustn't let them catch us – ever!' she cried. 'We must get beyond the Marsh!'

Her sudden changes of mood, and that inexplicable look, were nearly as baffling to John as her hasty speech had been on the day of his escape. He had to ask: 'But if Old Potter knows the way through the Marsh, why can't we go now? Why have we – and the others, too – got to wait?'

'We're not old enough yet, for one thing.' Her tone was still light, but the look had faded. 'And they – the people beyond the Marsh – want new recruits who can do the full work. They've got children, young ones, so they want only grown-ups. And we've got to show that we would fit in.'

'But if we can do the work,' John began –

'There's a lot more to it than that!'

But before John could ask her what she meant, Janet's mood had abruptly become one of warning, and he saw that they were approaching where the Old Way was crossed by a lane curving down from the hills. They went on cautiously, but no sound came from the lane except the cawing of rooks high in a group of trees clinging to the slope.

By the time they had regained the safety of the may-hedges John felt less inclined to press his questions. Janet's changes of mood – the way she jumped from delight at the may-blossom to anger at the Party and from that to excitement at the prospect of going beyond the Marsh even though she knew that was years away – were more than puzzling. And, John remembered uneasily, for all her apparent light-heartedness she had voted for Hugh to be denied such a future.

If there was such a future, John added to himself as he walked beside her. Again the conversation he had overheard between Helen and Gwen had come back to him; and he realised that, during her months at Base, Janet too must surely have heard such doubts as Helen's expressed – indeed, she might have been in the girls' recess while Helen and Gwen had been talking. Had she, he now wondered, been also trying to ignore those doubts, been clinging to the hope that they could be sure of their freedom beyond the Marsh even though the Party clearly knew of the place? For several paces he thought to ask her directly, bluntly; but he edged away from the idea, unsure if she could face such an open expression of the fragility of their hopes, or if he could face it himself.

At last he asked: 'Who decides when we're old enough to go on? Does Old Potter, or is there someone else?'

'Old Potter would have to agree that we're suitable. And the others would vote, of course. . . And you'd have to be asked.'

'Asked? Who by?'

'You never know; I might ask you.'

'You?' As he spoke John remembered Gwen had spoken of Eric wanting her to ask Ewan rather than Duncan.

Janet began, a laugh in her voice: 'Don't worry. It's years yet –'

She broke off as they both heard a van starting up. They were nearing another crossing lane. The noise had come from behind the hedge as if a patrol had been standing, hidden.

They slipped into cover as the van, after only a short way, abruptly stopped. For several moments no sound came from it. At last Janet whispered: 'If we have to separate, work your way round beyond them. An ash-tree sticks out of the hedge further along. I'll get there.'

Still there was no sound from the van. It was as if the men had seen them and were waiting for them to show themselves again. Then, abruptly, the van started and began to grind up the hill.

They stood a while longer, John wondering if one of the men could have got out unheard and was now trying to reach them along behind the hedge. But the birds were still fluttering about it, were not rising in a quick cloud as if alarmed.

Janet said: 'We'll have to risk it.'

They edged to the lane. It was empty and the sound of the van had died away up the hill. Janet ran across to the cover of the next stretch of hedge. As John joined her he asked: 'Why did they stop if they hadn't seen us?'

'If Eric and Duncan can't find out how Party-men think, how can we?' She spoke as if they had not a few moments before been standing tense and afraid. As a curve of the hedge hid them from the lane, she seemed to resume her bewildering excitement. 'If only we could go on at once!' Catching John's surprise, she added quickly: 'Of course we can't. They'd say we're not sure enough...There's the ash-tree!'

She ran towards a grey-green tree rising out of the hedge, squirmed under the hanging branches and then scrambled up through the tangle that climbed the sudden rise. Under a beech-tree she stopped to sit on one of its gnarled roots. 'Now we've got to wait until he comes,' she told John as he struggled up to her. A blackbird, startled by their sudden appearance, flew squawking away. 'He'll soon know someone's here,' she added.

Her mood had quietened. She suggested having another

potato-and-bean cake as they waited. 'I'll be glad when more new vegetables come in,' she went on. 'Old Potter says that before nineteen ninety-seven, people had all sorts of things to eat, things we don't have at all. Some of them came from places far away, he said, kinds of food that we can't grow.'

'How could they?' John asked. 'I mean, some of our harvest – when I was at the House – went to the Party; I suppose they sent it to other places, but we grew it all.'

'It's something to do with money,' Janet said. 'I couldn't understand all he said, but the people who grew the food somehow exchanged it with the people who made things. And they made all kinds of things, Old Potter says: brighter clothes and better tools and those things the duty-women talk into, and machines like Duncan tries to find out about and – and music!'

'Music?' John could not recall having heard the word.

'Yes! I've never told you, have I? Old Potter can make it; and it – it's different from any noise you've ever heard!'

John was more baffled. 'But what's that got to do with – with people getting food they didn't have to grow?'

Janet laughed. 'It was one of the things they had before nineteen ninety-seven.' And then: 'I wonder if it'll be like that beyond the Marsh. I wonder if we'll have nicer cloth and music and – and better food, better even than we had at our House.'

'Will he tell us about such things today?' John asked.

Janet started up. 'Here he is!' she said.

The man was only a few paces away, but more than the suddenness of his appearance held John's eyes. Old Potter was stockily built though his shoulders drooped with age so that the head under its thick, grizzled hair was thrust forward; and the face looked older than any John had ever seen. Sharp stabs of lines between the thick brows and a crease on either side of the wide mouth gave an impression of aged sadness until, as the man recognised Janet, every line seemed suddenly to twist in greeting.

'Let me remember.' Old Potter's voice was husky. 'You're Janet from Eric's group over near Watford: that's right, isn't it? And this. . .?'

'He's John,' said Janet. 'He came from Eric's old House. He's new.'

The old eyes rested on John's face and, though the man still smiled, there was also calculation in his look. 'You're young, too,' he commented; and then to Janet: 'You've voted on him, of course?'

'Oh yes – the other day.'

Old Potter nodded. 'Come along in.'

He led through a thicket of blackthorn, and then disappeared into a doorway so screened as to be all but invisible. John followed Janet into a small brick-walled room, built into the slope of the hill, low and with wide slits of windows that gave a view over the land spreading beyond the hedges of the Old Way. There was space for only three or four people at most.

A chair, its cover tattered, stood in one corner. As Old Potter eased himself into it, John squatted beside Janet on the floor.

'You'll have news for me,' said Old Potter.

'We have,' replied Janet quickly. 'The Party: they've found Base. They made a search – three patrols together. And since then the patrolling's stopped!'

'Three patrols?' The old man sounded more surprised than concerned.

'And Eric saw one of the Party-men go into Base. He must have seen we were living there – we didn't have time to hide everything! But they didn't wait inside for us. . . Eric wants to know where we can go if they look like trying to catch us. He thinks they might wait for a few days to see if we dash off to another group.'

'They might try that.' Old Potter frowned. 'Did they touch anything, do you know?'

'Not as far as we could see,' Janet replied. 'We all looked everywhere. The Party-man must have just gone in and out again.'

'Did he leave anything behind?'

'We didn't see anything,' Janet began; but John remembered the little metal box that Duncan had found. 'He said that it might have been there among his things for a long time,' he told Old Potter. 'But he'd never noticed it before.'

'What was it like?'

'Small and flattish; and I think there were some slits in one side and –'

Old Potter's look had sharpened. 'It's a long time since I've seen one,' he said slowly. 'It sounds as if it could have been a bugging device.'

' "Bugging"?' The word snatched John's thoughts back to the time when he had lain in his hide and heard the Party-men speaking below him. It brought, too, fear like that he had then felt.

Janet stared at him and then back at Old Potter. 'What is it?'

'They used to have them before nineteen ninety-seven,' the old man said. 'I've never heard that the Party has found how to use them, but. . . They're for listening. You put one in a room and then you have what's called a receiver outside so you can hear what's being said inside.'

John was staring at the old, lined face. 'You mean they might have heard what we were saying?'

The old man shrugged. 'If it was a bugging device.' His tone was almost indifferent. 'There's plenty of places near your Base where they could have hidden, and if they happened to be listening in. . .'

'They might have heard – everything!' Janet cried.

As if not hearing her alarm, Old Potter asked: 'I suppose you didn't think to destroy it?'

'Duncan was going to look at it; but Eric was more concerned about us coming down here to you! They might have heard that!'

'And there was Hugh!' John added.

Still the old man looked unconcerned. 'Hugh?' he asked.

Janet began impatiently: 'He'd stolen before. He made out the pig had strayed so we had to vote to send him to the Island. . . But if they know about us coming here –'

But Old Potter appeared preoccupied with the thought of Hugh. 'He was the one with fair hair, wasn't he? A useful one, good at trapping, but like hunters always wanting to go his own way. And he wanted too much, too soon. I had my doubts. . . but by the time I met him, Eric and the others had voted.' The old eyes, now clouded, turned to John. 'So you had to vote to send him to the Island? It must have been about the first time you'd had to vote. You didn't find it easy, did you?'

'No, but I –' John stopped himself, unsure what the old man was meaning. Was he assuming that he had condemned Hugh to the Island and thought him unduly harsh?

Old Potter went on: 'It had to be done, and you have to accept it. It's the fairest way to decide. What's the alternative: to be forced to accept others' decisions, to change one party for another? No, you must vote as you think, even if it comes hard sometimes.'

John could not grasp what the old man meant; and, like Janet, he was wanting to concentrate on their immediate danger. He found himself repeating: 'They may have heard Eric telling us about coming here!'

The possibility did not appear to disturb Old Potter. 'Did you see any patrols on the way?' he asked.

'Yes!' Janet told him. 'One at the last lane across the Old Way!'

'Only one? Then they're not out searching for me.' Catching John's astonishment at his unconcern, the old man went on: 'They know I'm somewhere around here. They could send out a dozen patrols to find me if they thought I was worth it.'

John knew he was staring at him, trying to understand. Unexpectedly Old Potter smiled. 'Does that surprise you? The Party knows about me – not everything, of course, but enough to catch me if they wanted to. It's like you at your Base. They know you're living there; they could have caught the lot of you if they'd been told to. But, instead, they're watching – and listening, too, perhaps.'

Janet began: 'But why –?'

'Orders,' said the old man, and again John recalled the Party-men below his hide. 'That's how the Party works. The District Leaders: they decide what's to be done and then they tell the Party-man, and the duty-men too if it concerns them. They must have told the Party-men to find out where you were but not to catch you. . . It's hard to be sure what the Party is up to sometimes,' he added. 'Perhaps the Leaders themselves aren't always sure.'

As John frowned at that, Janet said again: 'We must get back and warn them. They may say something –'

'If you dash back without any rest, you'll run into a patrol,' the old man warned. 'You'd better wait until it's near dark and get back when they'll be expecting you. Then, if anything's happened and your Base isn't safe, one of the others would surely wait and warn you.'

Janet still looked uneasy, but John felt the danger in her alarm. And they had not yet found out all Eric needed to know. 'We may have to leave Base, Eric says,' John reminded Old Potter. 'Do you know anywhere that we could go to?'

The old man considered for a few moments. 'There's a place over at Wallingford. They left a week or two ago. The Party's not likely to look there again for a while.'

'Do you mean they caught them?' asked Janet.

'I've heard only that they've gone,' the old man replied. 'Anyway, it's too far if you're hoping to gather your crops later on. Wendover would be nearer, though they couldn't take all of you. Tell Eric that you may have to split up: some to Wendover, the others. . . Markyate would do for a few weeks, until somewhere safer can be fixed up. Can you remember that?'

'Yes,' said John, holding the unfamiliar names in his mind.

Old Potter glanced at the sack John had carried. 'What's that?' he asked. 'Is it potatoes you're wanting to exchange for fat or meat?'

'It's some of the first carrots and turnips as well,' John told him, opening the sack.

'They'll make a change. I've caught only one rabbit in ten days. What are you wanting?'

'Helen's getting low on fat.' Janet spoke impatiently, as if she wanted to concentrate on their dangers. 'And Eric says he may send on a pair later.'

Catching her tone, Old Potter said: 'You've nothing to gain by dashing back before time.'

'But they may say something, not realising —!'

'What are they likely to say? Surely Eric doesn't go blabbing where other groups are?' The old man glanced at John. 'Have you heard a name mentioned in the weeks you've been living at your Base?'

John shook his head. He had overheard Eric speaking of 'keeping in touch', and had guessed that he was referring to other groups; but never had he heard the whereabouts of any. 'But I've heard about going "beyond the Marsh",' he said. 'If the Party-men heard about that. . .'

The hint of a smile had come into the old man's eyes. 'The Party knows about that,' he said.

John's surprise was prompted more by Old Potter's easy acceptance than by his admission; and he heard more of protest than alarm in Janet's voice as she exclaimed: 'But it's years and years since they went there! If they knew that the people have gone back again —?'

Old Potter interrupted gently: 'It's as I was saying: orders from the Party Leaders. They must have decided to leave the people there — at least for the time being.'

Janet persisted: 'But since the river flooded they can't get their vans there, can they?'

'They could get there if they decided to. They could re-build the bridges —'

'Then why don't they?'

The old man seemed to draw back at the question. 'Think what would happen if the people there tried to stop them.

It might start the troubles again. . . or have you forgotten what I told you about before nineteen ninety-seven?'

'You mean about all the fighting and – and destroying?' asked Janet. 'And how the Party made everyone work, and doped them? Of course I remember!. . . But that was years and years ago! And I don't see what it's got to do with – I mean, if the Party can get beyond the Marsh. . .'

'You'd better listen while I explain to John,' said Old Potter. 'It's not until you understand what happened that you can begin to guess how the Party Leaders might be thinking. I say "might"; I don't know for sure. Perhaps the Leaders don't know for sure themselves. . . You're not feeling too sleepy to listen for a while, are you?'

'No,' said John quickly; and, seeing the wrinkles tightening about Old Potter's eyes as the old man collected his memories of nineteen ninety-seven, he recalled how, during that long night below his hide, he had wondered if Old Potter's knowledge of that far-off time might provide some answers to understanding all that still baffled him.

'First you must know how people lived in those days. . .'

John tried to hold on to every word; yet so strange were many of the ideas Old Potter spoke of that soon bewilderment was intruding. For the man told that before nineteen ninety-seven people had lived very differently from the way John knew. Only some of them had produced the essential food; most of the people had done other work – the old man spoke of 'manufacturing' and 'providing services' – and had somehow bought the food they hadn't time to grow, some of it 'from abroad', whatever that meant. And by such a strange way of living, the people had contrived to 'enjoy a much higher standard of living than we have now', a phrase that hinted of what Janet had meant when she had spoken of 'brighter clothes and better food'.

But, the old man went on, such plenty had brought not satisfaction and well-being, but quarrelling and violence. John stared his incredulity as Old Potter told of the people coming to believe that 'it was unjust that some should live much better than others', and arguing that 'the rewards of work should be more fairly distributed', while other people 'insisted on their freedom to spend what they had earned.' John felt himself groping for meanings in the strange phrases and stranger ideas while the old man told of a 'growing confusion of beliefs, some people believing they knew how to put things right, others believing that their solutions were the only true ones. Of course, if they'd been as democratic as they pretended to be, they'd have voted on it, and stuck to that vote. . .'

John tried to keep his mind on the now-familiar word, but Old Potter was going on, was telling of groups of people 'calling meetings and staging protests to put their ideas over. Another lot of people, believing differently, would be breaking up their meetings, and fighting would start. . . The violence seemed to feed on itself. It went on and on until it became so widespread that work was interrupted, factories had to close, the distribution of food was prevented, and the essential services couldn't function. . .' Again John missed a few sentences as he struggled to understand. 'More and more people took to violence, not to put things right but to get what they needed – food, above all! They banded together to rob and attack those who hindered them. They got weapons – and bombs! You don't know about such things. They kill and destroy. With them the people fought: blowing up roads to stop the food lorries, raiding farms and stealing the stock for food, breaking into shops and warehouses where there was still something to steal. And they fought amongst themselves for what they got. . . When a fire was started it spread because the firemen couldn't deal with it – the water supply might have been damaged or a crowd might hamper them. When people were injured – the hospitals couldn't cope with so many injured! Then disease spread, and hunger too. . . and that increased the fears, the violence. . . '

Staring into Old Potter's face, John saw that every crease was twisted with hideous memories, telling him more than the unfamiliar phrases could. . . until there flashed into his mind Ewan speaking about the buildings around Base. Ewan, too, had told of people 'fighting among themselves' and 'destroying buildings', and had linked his words with the ruins they could then see. And there were other such ruins lining the way John had walked to a Celebration, and being cleared at Chesham as he and Janet had walked through last night. And she had come from a place called Tring: was that, too, in ruins? And Ewan and Helen had come from other places, and there might be more than they had seen among the hills and on the flat land reaching out below the little building in which they now were.

John became aware that Old Potter was explaining about the Party, and speaking as if he had himself been a member. 'We had to take over,' he insisted. 'We had a means of stopping the violence. . . I was what was called a chemist, working for a firm that made drugs and medicines. As the violence grew we made and imported more and more tranquillisers – people demanded them to stop them from thinking too deeply about what was happening. We had some new ones, very powerful ones, and as distribution broke down we had large stocks on our hands. In sufficient doses those tranquillisers could so quieten people that they wouldn't be able to act violently. . .

'We put it in the food at first. Some Party-members knew people in some of the ports, others took over what stores remained. . . As they distributed the food they doped it, so that first in one area, then in another, the fighting began to die down. Gradually the Party spread its activities further. I don't know the details; I was too busy making the stuff. The Party must have got extra supplies from abroad; some members, I know, had contacts. . .

'As the people began to quieten, the Party set them to work. It was an immense task, so much had been destroyed. We had to concentrate on absolute essentials: getting food crops sown, gathering such sheep and cattle as had survived, rebuilding only what was needed immediately, restarting factories to make necessities. It took years before we had the work organised to provide more than the barest minimum. We had so much to do that we did not realise that the tranquillisers were even more effective than we had thought. . .

'I'd reckoned that, after a few years, we'd stop using the stuff. But others in the Party said that so many people had suffered that to relax too soon would revive the old quarrels, bring back the violence. They argued that it would take a generation or two before we could relax. After a lot of discussion it was agreed to cut down the doses a little – only a little – and meanwhile they set about reorganising the way people lived. It was, they said, dangerous to let people live in separate homes, in families; it was necessary for the people to live where they could at all times be kept under control. You know about that.'

For a few moments the old man sat staring, unseeing. Then, as if recalling what had prompted his tale, he went on: 'The Party Leaders: even now, so long afterwards, they wouldn't willingly risk that the fighting and violence might start again. They could go beyond the Marsh; they could rebuild the bridges, clear the roads, drain the land. But if the people already there tried to oppose them. . . Of course the Party could overcome them. But even a small conflict might stir up the old hatreds among those whose memories stretch as far back as nineteen ninety-seven, it might set off the younger ones who've never known how violence breeds violence. If the people beyond the Marsh are not a danger to the Party. . . I don't know for sure. It's hard to know, sometimes, how the Party Leaders may be thinking. . .'

Old Potter shook his head. 'Perhaps I should have stayed in the Party and kept on trying to persuade them. But some were so intent on keeping the people quiet; they could not understand that the young ones, growing up, had to know what had happened – so that they would also know the dangers. That's why people like you have got to know!. . . And it seemed to me that some Party Leaders were more concerned to hold on to the power they'd got than to do what was best. So I broke away – I had to! I couldn't go on working with them, doping the people, never letting them face up to what had been! You can't go on living in a way you don't believe in, you've got to hold on to your own beliefs as, maybe, you've been coming to find out. . . And, besides, there was another danger in keeping the people ignorant. The fighting and the horror: they were only part of the way people had lived before nineteen ninety-seven. They had done wonderful things, too! They could manufacture all kinds of things that made life easier and richer and fuller. They could make machines so that they could travel wherever they wanted to, and other machines that told them what was happening miles away. They made machines that worked for them, taking away the drudgery so that they could live in comfort. They had all kinds of food to help them to keep healthy, and they –'

'And Music!' added Janet so suddenly that John and Old Potter stared at her.

'You've remembered!' The old man's face, a moment before twisted with bitter memories, had at once softened with delight. John's stare became incredulous. Old Potter had been explaining, had been giving him a glimmer of understanding; and then, as if her mind had bounced away from all the old man had been saying, as if she'd also forgotten the dangers to Base, Janet had remembered the Music – whatever that was! And, as suddenly, Old Potter appeared so pleased that he had forgotten what he had been talking about!

'You'll not remember what it was called,' he was saying to Janet.

Incredibly Janet began: 'It's about a shoe –'

The old man's chuckle added to John's bewilderment. 'Schubert: he wrote it. It's called "Impromptu".'

He had opened a large flat box on a stool beside him, and began to wind a handle. 'This was old when I was your age,' he said, though why he should think that interested them was beyond John's reasoning. 'Luckily it doesn't need electricity,' the old man added, moving a switch. A black disc inside the box began to revolve. As if noticing John's consternation at the abrupt change of subject, he went on: 'It may help you to understand more. People used to like music. Many people –'

He broke off as the disc on the box gave out a scraping noise; and then, above it, John caught sounds such as he had never heard. His bewilderment rising afresh, he at first recalled the rhythmical noise that had sent the boys of his House prancing about at a Celebration. But Old Potter's noise was in an indefinable way utterly different. Above a running, ever-changing sequence of little sounds came out slower, stronger ones, at once gentle and penetrating. They seemed to seep into John's being, to still his near-anger that Janet should have deflected the old man's talk, to soothe and at the same time to stir unfamiliar feelings deep within him. He knew that Old Potter was smiling with an almost child-like delight, and that Janet's eyes were bright; but all his attention was held by the sounds. On and on they went, rising, falling, breaking into soft joyousness, fading to a half-sad whisper, reviving again. John felt as if the sounds were doing more than dissolving his consternation; they seemed to be easing the feeling of horror that the old man's story had brought.

Above the gentle, running little sounds, the more insistent ones swelled to a climax and then, fading, died away. Old Potter turned the switch. 'How did you like that?' he asked, smiling. 'Has it made you sleepy? You'd better have a nap so that you'll be ready when the time comes to go back.'

At that Janet began to make herself comfortable on the floor; but John, though he also lay down, felt unready for sleep. As the soothing of the music ebbed, the horrors in Old Potter's tale began to reclaim his thoughts. He could only glimpse what had brought the conflicts and the violence – so much that the old man had said was far beyond his understanding – but he found himself again linking the story of destruction with the empty, ruined buildings he had seen. . .

He caught Old Potter's eyes on him and in their depth was a look of great sadness. The old man shook his head as if to say again that his tale had to be told and that it was imperative for John to have heard it.

Old Potter glanced at Janet already appearing asleep. With the hint of a smile, he whispered to John: 'You're finding it hard to doze off? Let's try the music again.' He moved the switch. 'Remember that the people before nineteen ninety-seven liked it too,' he added. 'The killing and the destroying – those were the bad parts. Many people enjoyed such music as this. . .'

Old Potter's voice faded as again the sounds began gently to take over the little room.

9

Return to Danger

JOHN awoke at Old Potter's touch. He looked up into the lined face smiling down at him; and then glanced at Janet. To his surprise she was still asleep.

Without the alive brightness of her eyes and the quick smile, her face looked less assured. A slight droop to her mouth hinted of uncertainty as if, John thought, in sleep a fear of disappointment was no longer masked by her liveliness. Again, as on their walk along the Old Way, he felt he was seeing more about her than he had noticed before.

The old man had followed John's glance. 'She's a lively little one,' he whispered. 'It would hurt her even more than most if she never got beyond the Marsh.'

At that, Old Potter's tale and what he had said about the Party surged into John's consciousness, a rush of impressions in which fear and puzzlement and alarm and hope were tangled, bringing sudden questions. He began: 'But if the Party can get there –'

'When your time comes you'll have to chance that they'll still be unwilling,' said Old Potter. 'And, for the present, you've more urgent things to be thinking of.'

Janet had awoken, was starting up. 'Is it time?'

'It'll be dark enough by the time you reach the lane up into the hills,' the old man told her.

John still felt the questions crowding; but as Old Potter glanced at him again, he caught a strained look on the lined face. 'Tell Eric to let me know what you decide,' the old man went on. 'I'll have the fat ready by then. You remember the places I said? Wendover and Markyate.' He turned away as if he did not wish to see them leave.

They did not speak until after they had scrambled down to the Way and had walked some distance along its grassy route. John was turning over in his mind what he could recall of Old Potter's talk. The old man's almost casual acceptance that the Party could go beyond the Marsh had revived his earlier fears. To be sure, Old Potter had also spoken of the Party Leaders being possibly reluctant to go and risk a revival of the horrors of long ago; but how could he be certain of that? Old Potter had himself said, more than once, how difficult it was to know how the Party might be thinking.

And the old man had been little concerned about the possibility that the box Duncan had found might be a 'bugging device'. Again John recalled the two Party-men below his hide. Whether or not that box was such a thing, they had clearly intended to use one. . .

He hardly saw the may-blossom, its whiteness even more dazzling in the last rays of the setting sun. Fear was taking hold of him, fear that never again might he see such a sight, that he might by some scarcely comprehensible means be trapped by the Party and become dulled again so that he would forget all the aliveness he had experienced during the past weeks. The shadows gathering under the may-hedges seemed threatening, as if they were concealing Party-men.

John did not notice that the sight was, incredibly, having the opposite effect on Janet, until she broke into his thoughts: 'It's even better than when we came!. . . Do you think Old Potter could have been right about that box Duncan found? It hadn't got any wires.'

John frowned. She was as she had been when they had come, her mood changing with startling abruptness. She went on: 'Duncan says that those telephone things had to have wires. Perhaps Old Potter had forgotten. He's so old —'

With a decisiveness that surprised him, John interrupted her. Whatever the Party might or might not be able to do, he felt a need to put an end to guesses and speculations, to regain a semblance of certainty, brief though it might be.

Back at Base they would have to move elsewhere and that, at least for a while longer, would keep them out of the Party's clutches. 'Whether that was a "bugging device" or not,' he said, 'they've had plenty of time to fix one up. Base has been left empty all day!'

Her look changed. Just for an instant, she appeared surprised that he should have so spoken; then her face went tight as if she, too, felt that the Party was gathering against them, endangering their wavering hopes.

When they reached the lane up into the hills, Janet did not pause to check the route. She was on, forcing herself up the steepening slope. By the time they were nearing the top the night was gathering under the beeches; but it brought no feeling of protection. Reaching more level ground Janet tried to quicken her pace; but as they neared the hill-top pond she suggested that they might get on faster for a short rest. Though they sat a while, eating the last of their cakes and scooping a few handfuls of water, John could feel no sense of refreshment, not the slightest relaxation. He felt, rather, that the dangers were massing, were coming nearer with every step they took towards Base.

Some hours later, as they were nearing the ridge above Chesham, they heard a van approaching. As always they slid into cover; but to John it seemed as if the patrol was scarcely looking, the van went so steadily past. Could the patrol have been not seeking to catch them but merely checking their route? As they resumed walking, John glanced at Janet, thinking to ask her what she thought; but the shuttered look on her face made him hold back the question.

The moon had set and the night was beginning to fade as they came over the hill above Base. Though Janet had kept trying to urge herself faster, their pace had slackened. As the first of the ruins loomed ahead, she stopped, peering through the thin light. John, too, looked towards the chimney rising beyond the dark cypress-tree. The signal was not warning them away.

'They must be inside,' Janet whispered, but she sounded unsure.

No noises other than those of birds waking to the day had reached them; yet John, too, felt uneasy. Party-men might be as skilled as he in avoiding notice; they could even now be waiting silently inside Base.

He asked Janet: 'Do you know any of the others' hides? If we could find one of them. . .?'

Janet shook her head. 'Helen's is down below Base, I know. I think Duncan's is over that way.' She waited, listening, through several seconds. At last she whispered: 'We'll have to risk Base. I'll go first. Give me a little while in case. . .'

She moved stealthily on. Watching, John saw that tiredness had stolen some of her skill. Once she stopped abruptly as, with unusual clumsiness, she brushed against an outreaching branch. But there was no responding hint of movement from the growth and ruins ahead. After some seconds she went on again.

John began to follow, his ears intent for any whisper of sound, his eyes searching for any hostile movement. He saw Janet reach the darkness under the tall cypress – and then suddenly stop, tense, peering towards the growth masking the entrance to Base. John, too, stood watching, ready for any hint. . .

She began to edge back towards him. John guessed that she must have seen or heard something telling that Base might be unsafe. After a few paces she again stood rigid in the cover of a thick hawthorn.

Again she waited through several moments. At last she turned towards John, but she did not resume her cautious walk. Instead she pointed first to herself, then at John, then towards the direction of his hide. John understood. She was going to make for his hide. They would have to lay up there –

She had slipped away before John suddenly remembered. He had broken the string which pulled down the rope; they could not gain the hiding-place under the roof. The alarming realisation sent him after her, intent on warning her and scarcely heeding in the greater danger that his urgency was causing him to blunder against low branches. Then, suddenly, he saw her stop again.

He knew that she must have seen danger ahead, but he had to reach her, to warn her. He saw her stiffen as he neared her, and guessed that she was alarmed that he should risk moving. Then as he reached her he, too, saw the van standing in a lane as if waiting for them to show themselves.

He knew that they had to turn back. 'It's no good,' he whispered. 'We can't use my –'

A movement from the van made them both start. At once there were other sounds about them as if the growth was hiding more than a single patrol. With a gasp Janet was off, crouching as she ran on towards John's hide.

She went a hasty, darting course, running from cover to cover only to turn aside as a fresh movement seemed about to impede her. She worked her way upwards to cross the lane above where the van stood, and then turned down through the cover beyond. Forcing himself after her, John heard more movements about them, seeming to be converging on them.

He caught up with her as she scrambled in through the window space. 'It's no good!' he hissed. 'I had to break the string! We can't get the rope!'

Janet stopped, turning on him a terrified, accusing stare; and then her face seemed to crumple as a voice from inside the building said: 'That's right. There's nowhere for you to run to.'

John glared past Janet at the bulk of the man standing in the darkness. He barely noticed the level voice, but he saw the man raise his head as he called to someone outside: 'Here are two more of them!'

* * * * *

For John the next two hours held a feeling of confusion in which alarm and fear were mingled with unexpected naturalness. As the man took them to a nearby van about which four or five men stood waiting, John felt a sense of unreality. He had imagined that Party-men, near-to, would look somehow different; yet, except that each wore a small version of the badge he had seen on the District Leader's tunic, the men appeared unremarkable. And one, as he told them to get into the open rear part of the van, added: 'You must be needing a rest.'

For a moment Janet looked as if she was going to refuse to get in, perhaps to try to run. But instead she cried out: 'We'll not tell you anything – whatever you do!'

The Party-men looked unconcerned. One of them, a broad man with a wide mouth, said: 'There's nothing to be alarmed about.'

They sat on wooden seats on either side of the van, with a Party-man beside each of them. John could not look at Janet. He knew she was holding her head high again, that the shattered look he had caught as the Party-man had spoken from the darkness below his hide had been replaced by determination. He knew, too, that if he had met her eyes he would have seen again her accusation. Janet believed that his carelessness had trapped them.

They were driven through the fading night to the Local Centre. On the way the two Party-men spoke easily, the broad one remarking on work that was going on alongside their route. 'It's taken long enough to get this place cleaned up,' he said, nodding towards where a ruin was being pulled down. 'They've cleared that patch at last,' he commented on a roadside field newly dug. Strengthening John's feeling of unreality, the man seemed to be speaking as much to him and Janet as to the other Party-man. But for the slightly gruffer tone, he might have sounded like Ewan talking about the need to free the water-pipe or move the loo-site.

As they drew near to the Local Centre, John noticed that the streets about it looked less ruinous than in his memories of walking to a Celebration. Despite the fear that was clutching him, he felt as if, during his years at the House, he had been able to see only the ruins, had never registered that among them stood buildings patched-up and made habitable.

They stopped at the doorway in the tower of the Local Centre. For a moment Janet held herself stiffly as if she was going to refuse to follow the broad Party-man as he got down from the van. 'Come on,' he said. 'We're not all night-birds like you. As soon as we've found somewhere for the pair of you, we'll be able to get some sleep.' As he opened the door to the Centre, he added to John: 'Have you had anything to eat recently?'

The question so surprised John by its ordinariness that he began: 'No, we haven't. At least –'

He caught Janet's glare, fierce with anger that he should even hint that he might accept anything from a Party-man. But the man seemed not to notice. 'I'll see what we've got. It won't be much at this time of night.'

Unlike at a Celebration only a few lights now lit the Local Centre; and yet John seemed to see the place more clearly than before. It was long and stone-built. A double row of sturdy pillars held up a high, dark roof. Beyond the pillars on either side was a wide, shadowy passage-way reaching to the walls along which were pointed windows whose coloured glass showed that outside the light was growing. Never before had John noticed the building's sombre dignity; though clearly built long ago, it did not suggest people living in little rooms and in family groups.

The broad-built Party-man led them to a small room partitioned from the passage-way. Switching on the light, he said: 'Wait in here. It's too early for the District Leader to be ready. I'll see if I can find something to eat.'

Again John felt the unreality of what was happening. At the mention of the District Leader there had flashed into his mind a vision of the man's alert eyes under their jutting white brows, and the disturbing quickness of his movements; and yet the Party-man had spoken as if the District Leader was not so alarming a person. . .

Then John caught Janet's wild-eyed stare at the door and realised that the man had locked them in. She began in a tense whisper: 'Don't you see what they're doing? They're trying to put us at our ease so that when they question us about the others and how we live, we'll give way! And thinking to eat their food! Don't you realise it'll be doped so that we'll be half-asleep when they question us?'

Even the sharp fear in her eyes and the tension gripping her were unable to penetrate John's feeling of unreality. He stood looking at her, hearing her words, knowing them to be probably true, and yet unable to share her fear. A vague idea, as yet too unformed to be put into words, seemed to be intruding. . .

'What are you trying to do?' Janet went on, fiercely. 'Do you want the others to be caught, too!'

John remembered. 'They've caught some of them,' he said in a voice that sounded casual to his own ears. 'Don't you remember that Party-man saying something about us being "two more of them"?'

His accepting tone as much as the reminder seemed to add to Janet's alarm. 'Where are they then? What are they doing to them? Not that they'd tell – anything!' The near-contempt in her tone told John she was almost assuming that he would tell. 'What if they have caught one or two? If they don't say anything – and we don't either! –'

A key turned in the lock. Janet held herself stiffly as a woman came in carrying a tray with beakers of milk and some bread and butter. Unexpectedly she smiled. 'It's all I can do so early,' she said, putting the tray on a kind of stone table. Then, catching Janet's defiant stare, she said: 'You may have to wait a little longer.' She nodded towards a bench against one wall. 'At least you'll be able to sit down,' she added as she went out.

The food made John aware that he was hungry. They had eaten little for two nights and a day. But Janet's warning stare, reminding that the food might be doped, held him back. He went and sat on the bench and, raising his eyes from the food's temptation, stared at a stone notice on the wall opposite. Still he felt that there was, just beyond his awareness, an idea, an explanation perhaps. . .

He realised that Janet, too, was looking at the stone notice, was making out the words on it. Puzzled, he began laboriously to read them. Many letters were so different from those he had learnt at Lesson Time that he scowled.

Janet started, her voice tense: 'Look! It says someone's died here. It says: "She left two Twin-Daughters and died, alas!" Is that why they've brought us here? To frighten us, to show us what they can do if we don't tell?'

Again John could not feel a quick response to her alarm. Staring at the stone, he found the words she had read near the foot of it. They were followed by what appeared to begin as a date but ended with a meaningless jumble of letters: 'APRIL the IX, MDCCLXXII'. Then, as Janet's wide eyes turned to another stone notice, John too began to search among their strange lettered phrases.

Janet pointed to another one. 'It's again about someone dying here!'

Her fearfulness seemed to be merging with his feeling of unreality. He stared around at the stone notices, caught sight of a short one, no more than a name and a date –

He had to read it twice before he understood. Then: 'Look! That one says: "Born July 19th 1807; Died May 14th 1837". That's years and years ago!'

Janet began: 'They must all have died here –'

John interrupted her. 'But don't you see? They're about people of long ago! They must have been here for years, long before nineteen ninety-seven!'

As she turned to him, John glimpsed through her fear surprise at his tone. But she still clung to an assumption that the Party-men were using the implications of the stone notices. 'They must have realised we'd see them when they locked us in here! They must have meant it as a threat –'

Again John interrupted her, his voice firm: 'Why should they want to kill us? What good would it do them?'

'But if they can't get us to tell them –!'

As if a mist was lifting, John found himself expressing the ideas that had been forming in his mind. 'What have we got to tell them that they don't already know? They've caught some of us, they know about Base. They may have been listening to what the others have been saying; and even if they haven't, Old Potter said that they can get beyond the Marsh if they decide to.'

He saw the wildness ebbing from her eyes as if she, too, was shedding the last remnants of her improbable hopes. 'What can they do to us?' John went on, seeming to think more clearly than he had ever done. 'They can send us back to our Houses, or – or make us work for them. But we know how to escape again. We know the water is doped. If we watch when the duty-men aren't looking –'

Janet's hopefulness was flickering afresh. 'Yes, we could! We could even tell other people. We could lead them to Old Potter! And if he's right about the Party not wanting to force the people already beyond the –'

The key turned again in the lock. The woman came in. Seeing the untouched food, she exclaimed: 'But you must be hungry! It's only milk – you've had it before – and bread and butter. . . and the Sub-Leader will be here soon.'

John looked at the food and then at Janet. He saw her fear returning, but he took a beaker of milk for her as well as for himself.

There was a sound outside the open door. 'Eat it up,' the woman said, offering the bread and butter. 'The Sub-Leader's here already!'

A Party-man came in, one they had not seen before. He was tall, with a lean, firm face, and a coloured strip under his badge suggested that he was senior to the other Party-men. 'You've given them something to eat?' he asked the woman. 'Good! We don't want them to be hungry when they get to District Headquarters.'

John recalled the other Party-man mentioning the District Leader, and again he saw in his mind the man's sharp eyes and his disturbingly alert movements.

The Sub-Leader glanced at him. 'There's no hurry,' he said. 'It'll not take an hour to get there.'

John tried to eat the bread and butter, but his mouth was suddenly dry. The comforting idea that, whatever happened, they could escape again began to dissolve. He could not look at Janet, but he knew that she, too, must be feeling the Party's hold tightening. With an effort he swallowed a mouthful and gulped some milk to ease it down.

'Ready?' the Sub-Leader asked. 'Come along then.'

Two more Party-men followed them as they walked to the door of the Local Centre. Outside, only a pace or two away, another van was waiting, one with its rear part enclosed like a windowed box with seats inside. One of the Party-men opened the door, the other stood so near that escape was impossible, though Janet flung a defiant stare at him as she got into the van. At the Sub-Leader's nod, John followed her in and, as the Sub-Leader took the seat beside the driver, the van door shut.

John was aware that Janet, too, was trembling as the van started up; but, unlike her, he could not summon any hint of defiance. As the van moved away from the Local Centre, he tried to cling to the hope that, whatever the Party decided, they could find a way back to freedom.

Not until they had gone some way did he begin to notice that most of the buildings they were passing were complete with roofs and windows. He saw that some looked less newly repaired than others, and recalled Old Potter talking of 'rebuilding what was needed immediately'. Again John was made very aware of how little, when living at his House, he had been able to see, to realise. . .

The Sub-Leader turned to them. 'Watch as we go,' he said. 'The District Leader will expect you to have seen all the work that's been done – and what's still to do.'

John was aware that Janet, too, was staring at the man with sharp surprise. 'Keep watching,' the Sub-Leader added. 'It will save the Leader having to explain so much.'

10

Journey towards the Future

AFTER only a few minutes' drive, they came out on to a much wider road, divided lengthways into two, reminding John of the roadway he and Janet had crossed on the evening of his escape. At the recollection of that occasion John felt fear wrenching at him. He hardly saw that several vans, some of them large, were passing along the wider road, until the Sub-Leader, glancing over his shoulder, commented: 'People had a lot more vans when this road was made.'

Again the man spoke easily, but his very naturalness added to John's fears. Not for several minutes could his eyes take in that the wide road was leading through a landscape where groups of buildings stood among fields with an occasional heap of rubble or a broken wall among bushes and trees suggesting that there had once been more of them. Now and again the road went under or over another. At one such point John saw that the road above looked to have been broken down and then rebuilt; and he recalled Old Potter telling of people blocking roads to stop food vans, and fighting. Further on he saw through a group of trees a tall building with blackness still showing above its window-gaps as if, long ago, it had been set on fire, and again he remembered Old Potter's tale.

Buildings became more frequent. John found himself leaning forward, staring, as they passed more and more groups of them set in cleared fields with crops growing and cattle grazing and, here and there, boys or girls working with a duty-man or woman standing by. But still he saw, now and again, areas tangled with growth out of which ruins rose. The sights seemed to submerge John's fears as his mind groped towards a realisation that once many people must have lived in the traces of buildings, far more people than those who now occupied the complete ones. He recalled having thought, as he had listened to Old Potter, that there must be other places than those he had seen up to then, other groups of ruined and deserted buildings; but he had been thinking of there being perhaps a few dozen of them, each in his imagination a group of a few short streets. Now, as the van went on and on through a landscape looking to have been reclaimed from ruin, he realised with horror that Old Potter had been trying to convey far more extensive devastation than he had visualised. He looked at Janet and saw that her face was tight as if she, too, was seeing what lay behind the sights.

And then they were passing many buildings all of which were in use. John saw men and women going into a long, low building and guessed that it must be one of those in which people worked for the Party. But the people looked as if undisturbed by having to go there; some even smiled a greeting to others as they met at the door. And then there were more people, men and women and children walking along beside the road, passing the large windows of buildings in which were lengths of coloured cloth and shining new cooking pans, and neatly draped, new-looking garments, and displays of food. John recalled Janet speaking of 'brighter clothes and better tools. . . and kinds of food we can't grow'; but at the same time his eyes were catching the way the people were walking with a persistence that reminded him of the duty-men and yet had not so ponderous a movement. He saw that the children ambled along, their faces placid and yet not so empty as those of the boys at his House. He caught sight of a little girl pointing out something in one of the large windows to the man and woman walking with her, and he recalled the phrase 'family groups'. Again he turned to Janet and saw on her face an incredulous look that matched his own feelings.

Taller buildings loomed up, each of them far loftier than

the tower of the Local Centre. John stared. Their very height seemed threatening and though each had six or seven rows of windows, they appeared as if they had once been even taller. As the van drew up outside one, all John's attention seemed held by the monstrous place. Even before he saw the notice at the door – DISTRICT HEADQUARTERS – he felt that its towering bulk symbolised the Party's power.

'Here we are!' Again the Sub-Leader spoke easily; and then, catching the expression on both their faces, as they got out, he added: 'You look as if you have seen something of what the District Leader hoped you would. That's a good beginning.'

John turned his eyes from the building to the man. What did he mean? Through his mounting fear, John was again aware of the tangle of impressions the journey had brought: the traces of ruin recalling Old Potter's tale of horror, the signs of rebuilding, the boys and girls working, the older people appearing relaxed as they went into work-places or passed the big display windows. What did it all mean? Was the District Leader expecting those sights to have impressed them with the extent of the Party's power? Had he wanted them to see how firmly the Party still held the people so that he and Janet would know how futile it was to continue to oppose the Party's wishes? Or was the District Leader preparing them for his condemnation of their continued 'disobedience', so that they would submit to a return to their Houses rather than face some more restricting place like the Island?

'Come along,' said the Sub-Leader. 'We mustn't keep him waiting. He's a busy man, you know.'

A Party-man was opening the door to the building, another was standing nearby and the driver of their van had got out and was looking towards them. Escape was impossible; yet John had to flash a look to see between the buildings standing opposite the fields reaching away into the distance. At the sight fear of captivity nearly overwhelmed him; somewhere beyond those fields he had become so vividly aware of the life around and inside him.

As he turned again to the door, he saw that Janet's dark head was again lifted as if her defiance had revived. With an effort, he steadied his legs to walk into the building.

They went up three flights of stone stairs, and with every step John felt that the place was crushing all hope out of him. . . until, as they crossed a landing, he recalled suddenly what he and Janet had been saying at the Local Centre just before the Sub-Leader had arrived. They knew how to escape again! Wherever they were sent, they would be able to avoid drinking too much of the doped water, and all the time they could be watching for an opportunity. . .

The Sub-Leader was taking them across a large room in which people were working at tables spread with paper or fingering clicking machines. Some glanced curiously at them, but John did not see them. He was trying to convey his thoughts to Janet, was trying by his look to remind her that whatever the District Leader might do to them, wherever he sent them, they could still escape. As the Sub-Leader tapped on a door, John turned almost desperately to her. 'We know,' he whispered. 'I told you in the Local Centre. . .'

Her tense face showed no response. She looked as if her determination to say nothing had driven all other thoughts out of her mind.

'Come in!' Through the closed door a voice John recognised made it impossible for him to say more.

The Sub-Leader opened the door and spoke of 'two from beyond Watford'. Still trying to cling to his hopes, John managed to steady himself and to walk into the room. Janet's chin was again lifted defiantly. She had not understood him; or had she shed all hope that they could escape again?

From behind a table on which were more papers, the District Party Leader was looking at them. Under the thick white hair, under the jutting brows, the sharp eyes seemed to reach towards them; and yet, though fear was shaking him, John was aware that the man did not appear so disturbingly alert.

'Sit down, both of you.'

The voice was quick, but not as sharp as in John's memory. Sitting, he felt a little steadier; he felt, too, his former sense of unreality returning. He could not yet realise that the change was in himself, that in the last weeks he had become accustomed to natural speech and so, by comparison, the District Leader sounded less alarming.

Janet was holding herself stiffly, her stare uncompromising; but the District Leader appeared not to notice. He glanced at a sheet of paper on the table. 'Let me see: you must be. . .' The blue eyes, less piercing than in John's recollection, lifted to his face. 'Chesham Four Hugh? No, you can't be. . . Ah yes: Watford Nine John, 227645. You ran away in April, I see, so you've been gone only a few weeks. And you?' He glanced at Janet. 'You'll be Tring Five Janet, 227673. You escaped in January. That wasn't a good time of year. How did you manage for food?'

Janet started at the question, so unexpectedly natural. From a flicker in the Leader's eyes John guessed that after a momentary surprise, her look had regained its defiance, telling that she was determinined not to respond to him.

'It's not important,' the Leader went on. 'I was just curious. Were you lucky at trapping rabbits, or had your potato crop been good?'

John began to feel that astonishment as much as determination was preventing Janet from answering. The man's quick eyes turned again to him. 'You were the latest recruit, I see. Did you know of the others before you escaped or did you meet them by chance?'

Again the man spoke so naturally that John opened his mouth to reply; but he was aware of the warning in Janet's stare.

'Perhaps you'll feel able to tell me later on,' said the Leader. 'There's nothing in our recordings about such details. Of course we haven't had much time to study your group. You were obviously intending to leave your headquarters, and that would have meant finding where you had gone and then again bugging the place; and as we had heard enough. . .'

The Leader paused, the white brows raised in question as he caught John's start at the word 'bugging'. The hint of a smile came into the quick eyes. 'I see you know something of what I mean,' he went on. He opened a drawer in the table and took out a small, flat metal box. 'But Duncan was wrong, wasn't he – about having to have wires, I mean. . . though I must admit that he's shown a lot of ingenuity with some of his other things. That periscope he rigged up: that was clever of him.'

He seemed to catch Janet's alarm but, instead of responding, he opened a flat box on the table. 'We use bugging devices with this machine. It's one of the many tricks left over from before nineteen ninety-seven that we've rediscovered. I'll show you how it works.'

The Leader pressed a switch on the box. At once not a single disc but two smaller ones began to revolve, and out came the sound not of music but of voices. A girl's voice was saying: ' ". . . told John to go." ' And then a man, sharply: ' "I'm not blaming – anyone!" ' Then a younger voice: ' "I saw him. . . at least I think it was Hugh. His hair was nearly white. I thought at first –" '

The Leader touched the switch and the voices stopped. 'It's a useful device, isn't it?' he said. 'About fifty metres from your headquarters one of our men was recording your conversations.' Then, as if concerned at Janet's alarm, he added: 'We're not going to force you to tell us what we want to know. We're not like that and, as you've heard, we don't need to.'

Consternation and fear were seizing John. He realised that the snatch of conversation had taken place immediately he had returned from the scatter on which he had overheard the Party-men. The Leader must have heard everything they had said since then! He must have heard about Hugh's stealing. Was he assuming that all of them –?

The Leader went on: 'I hope you kept your eyes open

as you came here. I hope you saw for yourselves how much damage was done before nineteen ninety-seven. I see, by the look on both your faces, that you know what I mean. There was a lot of damage, wasn't there?. . . much more than Mr Potter could possibly have told you.' As Janet stiffened at the mention of Old Potter, he added: 'You need not be worried about him. . . though as he is getting old, perhaps we should find somewhere more suitable for him. No doubt he tried to give you an impression of what had happened. Your journey here has, I hope, told you more of the story.'

The Leader glanced over his shoulder out of the window behind him. From the higher level, John saw stretching away a huge landscape dotted with buildings in groups. About the nearer ones were paved spaces with vans on them; further away were many groups of smaller buildings standing among fields – John saw distantly an orchard, and cattle grazing, and a field with what looked like potato-rows. 'Once nearly all that was built over,' the Leader said, and John caught a note in his voice that reminded him of Old Potter. 'As you can see, we've cleared it and turned much of the land to good use. It's been a long job, far longer than Mr Potter expected.'

He turned again to them. 'But that wasn't what I really wanted to talk to you about. There's another part of this recording which particularly interested us. Listen again.'

He turned the switch and the voices were suddenly gabbling, high-pitched. Then he slowed the revolving discs. Eric's voice, hard and bitter, came out: ' ". . . like all of us Hugh knows that the last thing we want to do is to appear as thieves, living on others' work. . ." '

Recognising the occasion, John felt a chill stealing through him. He stared at the machine, at once fascinated and repelled as it told of Hugh's trial. He caught Eric's bitter condemnation: ' "If he had been hungry and so had felt compelled to steal, any of us would have understood. . . But it is the pretence that we must think of, the way Hugh has tried to excuse what he knows to be wrong, the way he expects us to accept his pretence. We cannot live here together pretending to one another. We cannot, when the time comes, go beyond the Marsh and live among the people there. . ." '

Janet gave a half-stifled gasp as if, until that moment, she had still been clinging to a desperate hope that the Leader might somehow overlook. . .

But John's thoughts were reaching ahead, reaching towards the vote that had condemned Hugh.

' "Not him!" ' Hugh's cry came out of the revolving discs. ' "He's only a kid and he hasn't joined –" ' And then Duncan's voice so soft that John could hardly catch the words: ' "John's one of us now. . . You take one stick of each size. Hold them under the table. . . You do as you think. No one will know how you have voted. . ." '

Fear was gripping John afresh, banishing the sense of unreality. The Leader had heard everything. He must be assuming that John had been among those who had condemned Hugh to the Island; and Janet, John knew, had done so. That was why they had been caught, had been brought before the Leader. But if he told the man how he had voted –

Hugh's anguished voice cut through John's wavering hopes. ' "It's John – he's only a kid! – and Janet, she's always hated –" '

The Leader abruptly switched off the voices. In the sudden silence John heard within himself words surging up to tell the man that he had not condemned Hugh, that he was not to blame –

The Leader's look, slightly narrowed, seemed to hint of warning. John held back the words as the Leader said: 'It must have been very hard for you – for all of you – to vote on such a matter. You must have hated to give him such a severe punishment.' And then, as again John leaned forward to tell him: 'No,' the Leader added. 'I don't want to know how you voted. That is no concern of mine.'

As John stared uncomprehending, the man went on: 'What interests me, and all of us, is that you voted on such a matter, that you had worked out a way to settle such difficulties. As I understand it, you have been living for some time – for three or four years for the older ones – working together and sharing your food, and managing to produce most of your other needs. Other groups of what we used to call Lost Ones have tried to do the same; but most of them took to stealing when the food ran short, and often they fought among themselves. I wish that all Lost Ones had as good a record as you, but unfortunately –'

As if unable to listen more, Janet suddenly blurted: 'What are you going to do with us? You know all about what we've been doing! Are you going to send us to a House or – or worse?'

Surprised by Janet's outburst, the Leader's look sharpened, and yet John thought he glimpsed in the alert eyes not so much anger as puzzlement. Janet went on, her voice shriller: 'You – you're playing with us! It's like a game to you! It's nothing to you that we've tried to live better –'

'No!' The Leader's voice, suddenly penetrating, stopped her open-mouthed. 'It is no game!'

The Leader drew himself back in his chair as if moving away from his own sharp interruption. At last, his tone easier: 'You must try to understand, otherwise I cannot ask you to help us. Mr Potter has told you a little, only the beginning. . .'

John missed a sentence or two as he tried to grasp the implications of the phrase: I cannot ask you to help us.

'. . . all the ruin that was left, not only to buildings but to people's lives. What you have seen on your way here, what you can see from that window – that is, you might say, only the shell of what we have had to do; the inside of it, the living part, you can't see. Mr Potter has told you how we got control; but, because he cut himself off so soon, he has never realised that even our methods did not quench the old bitternesses. When we tried to relax, the old fears and hatreds revived; some parents even passed them on to their children. . . It has been a far longer task than any of us guessed, and all the time we have had to keep the essential work going, to maintain supplies, to rebuild; for without that, nothing else could be achieved. . .

'When people started escaping we hoped they would find how to live together – but they didn't! The old quarrels broke out again, and we had to bring them back. . . But more recently, for nearly ten years now, some have been managing better. They have revived old villages and are working the land about them; they've even built workshops to make the equipment they need. They're learning to live together because, although they're too young to remember, they have come to see, as from a distance, something of what happened. Among others, Mr Potter has in his own way helped with that.'

John realised that Janet was leaning forward, her eyes intent on the Leader's deeply lined face.

'But I must warn you,' the Leader went on, 'that there are many in the Party who are not convinced that these new settlements will survive. They think we should go on as we have been doing for at least another generation. It will be up to young people like you to prove them wrong.'

'People like us?' echoed Janet in an incredulous whisper. She flashed a look at John, a look of mingled astonishment and hope. And then, turning again to the Leader: 'Do you mean that we – that you might let us go beyond the Marsh after all?'

'Not there exactly.' The Leader spoke gently as if to forestall Janet's disappointment. 'The people there have as much as they can deal with at present. But beyond Oxford there's good land, and some of the villages are still intact. One of your groups – the one from Wallingford – are going there; like you, they've learnt how to live together and how to share the work and the supplies, and – above all – how to deal fairly with those who do not fit in. Like you, they've had the courage to make their own decisions and – even more important – to keep to them.'

Beginning to understand, John felt hopefulness stirring in him, the hopefulness he had felt when first he had heard of 'beyond the Marsh'. He could go on, not living as they had done in hiding and uncertainty, but growing more and more aware of the life about and within him, and of his own understanding too.

As if still not daring to believe, Janet began: 'Do you mean that we might be able to go. . .?'

The Leader smiled quickly. 'Why not? You have shown that you can live with others. . . Really, you are both a little young still; but as your friends have agreed to go –' He caught Janet's surprise. 'Yes,' he added. 'Hemel Ewan and Chesham Helen have agreed, and so have Tring Gwen and Aylesbury Duncan.'

'Gwen and Duncan!' Janet exclaimed.

Amused understanding lit the Leader's eyes. 'Yes,' he said. 'Duncan has agreed to go with Gwen.' He turned again to John. 'There's something I must mention to you. As you may have realised, it is usual in these new settlements for the people to join in pairs, as in what you have come to call "beyond the Marsh". In the old days the man used to ask the girl. Nowadays, the practice is the other way round – you'll come to see that's not unreasonable as the woman will have to bear the children. I've not heard of any pairs splitting up after they've joined a settlement; it seems that being able to see so clearly what they are working for helps. I suppose, if things really didn't work out. . .'

Janet asked: 'Do you mean that Helen and Ewan, and Gwen and Duncan will be allowed to breed someday?'

The Leader stared his astonishment. 'Surely you don't think –!' He shook his head. 'How some of those old stories persist! We didn't realise at first that our doses might have such an effect, though a sudden rise in the population would have added to our difficulties in the early days. But for some years now all workers, when they're old enough and ready to take on the responsibility of a family home. . . You must have seen some of them on your way here!'

'Then they were family groups!' exclaimed Janet, and John knew that she looked quickly at him.

But another thought had occurred to John. 'Eric?' he asked the Leader.

The man's smile faded. 'We haven't contacted him yet. It may be better if we don't, for a while. He is – how can I put it fairly? – too rigid in his beliefs to settle readily. He does not want to understand, not yet.' He glanced at the paper before him, and added: 'I think you'll both agree that Chesham Hugh is not ready.'

'What will happen to him?' John asked.

'We shall have to send him to a House, at least for the time being. But he knows how to get away, and perhaps he has learnt not to make the same mistake again.'

As if she still could not fully believe, Janet asked: 'The others: they've agreed to go?'

The Leader nodded his white head. 'And four other pairs from Wallingford and three from Banbury. We're thinking of making it possible for others; we'd like twenty or so pairs, enough to start a sizeable village. There are young people working in factories who seem more fitted for such a life. They won't have had your experience, of course; but with help from people like you they could learn. . .'

Again John caught in the man's eyes a hint of sadness underlying his optimism that matched a look he had seen on Old Potter's face. Then, hearing the encouragement in his voice, John felt his own hopefulness strengthening afresh. Looking beyond the Leader, he saw out of the window the many buildings standing among the cleared land, and the animals grazing, and the orchard with its apple-trees pale with blossom, and the crop-fields trim and thriving where once ruined buildings must have stood. He saw, too, among the groups of buildings larger ones which he guessed to be work-places, and rows of smaller ones which must be family homes. And in his mind the man's look and the sight out of the window seemed to merge, and he felt that he could in time come to understand.

He knew that Janet had turned to him as if expecting

him to speak. But it was the Leader who added: 'I hope what I've said will help you. If you want to go back to living as you were, the door is open. You may prefer such an adventurous life, at least while you're young. If, on the other hand, you'd like to take a firmer hold on the future in a new settlement, the door is open to that, too.'

'Oh yes!' said Janet. 'To go with the others and – and start a new settlement!'

The Leader smiled. 'And you, Watford Nine John?'

Just for a moment John hesitated. The Leader's words had recalled the many awarenesses that had come to him during his first days as a Lost One: the feeling of life about and inside him, the awakening to the others' aliveness, and the hopefulness that had sprung up in him when he had believed that such new, exciting experiences could go on. And, linking and holding together such a vivid way of living, there had been the thrill of evading the patrols, of testing his new-found feeling of escape. Yet, below such exhilarating recollections, John knew that such a way of living was an illusion, scarcely more than a game.

'Yes,' he said. 'I must go too!'

Smiling, the Leader stood up. 'I'll let you know as soon as everything is arranged. For a few days you'll have to live at your Local Centre, but I'll keep it as short a stay as I can.'

He seemed to catch a lingering uncertainty in Janet's smile. 'The Music?' she asked. 'Will we be able to have, in the new settlement. . .?'

'Has Mr Potter still got that old disc?' exclaimed the Leader; and then, shaking his head: 'Sometimes I envy him the time to be able to sit and listen. . . Yes! You can have music there. A lot of it has survived – and many other things than you yet know of!'